CACHING OUT

ISBN: 978-0-692403-98-3

Third Edition

CACHING OUT

A NOVEL
TAMMY CHEATHAM

Dedication

*To Angie and Alicia, my sisters in crime
and to my Lillie who always believed.*

Prologue: July 1980

"No Mama, I ain't seen that old dog anywhere. I'll go look for him before Daddy gets home." Clutching a purple Popsicle in one hand, the boy looked up at his mother. Smiling at her with chocolate eyes, the dark haired boy walked out of the sunny yellow kitchen letting the screen door slam shut behind him.

He'd seen the dog. In fact, he knew just where to find the mangy mutt. Bay was his daddy's favorite hunting dog, a blue tick hound with big feet and long silky ears scarred by the raccoon and bobcat that he'd hunted over the years. He licked the last of the sticky purple syrup off the wooden stick, and stuck it in his back pocket.

"Well, he ain't gonna hunt no more, Daddy." Walking through the backyard, the boy slipped into a copse of pine trees that he was sure could touch the sun on a cloudless day. He worked his way through the trees, and skipped to where he'd left the dog hours before. Sliding down on a cushioned bed of pine needles that smelled like his mother's kitchen on mopping day, he crossed his legs Indian style and reached over to stroke the dog's head, softly rubbing between his soulful eyes; eyes already turning cloudy with death. "I had to do it boy, I just had to. Don't worry none, you won't be lonely 'cause I got a nice place for you right by the others."

Chapter 1: Present Day

From the shadow of an old, red brick building, the man watched. Watching was almost his favorite part.

Across the street sat a neat, one story house with window boxes overflowing with red and yellow spring blossoms. A dark blue police cruiser bearing the Pine Ridge Police Department emblem on its side was parked in front. The blinking lights pulsed, sending ribbons of red and blue shooting across the lawn and onto the stark whiteness of the house. Parked behind the car was an ambulance. He could have told them that they wouldn't need it, not for this one, but instead he slid further into the shroud of darkness. Even though all the lights in the house were on, he still saw the flashing of crime scene cameras as they photographed his latest masterpiece.

Too bad you didn't get to record it, too. A uniformed cop stepped out of the house and over to the railing that surrounded a small, wrap-around porch. The muted light from a fixture near the front door of the house illuminated the young cop's face, pale and grim. Pushing past a planter of ferns suspended over the porch and bracing himself on the railing, the officer bent with his head over the side of the porch.

"Come on cop, let it go. You'll feel so much better if you just puke and get it over with," the man in the shadows muttered. A hint of humor pushed one corner of the man's mouth upward. He really wanted to see the cop puke.

Minutes turned into hours and still he waited. The need to see her body being brought out twisted inside him, forcing him to rock back and forth on his heels. Softly chanting, the man declared, "It won't be long now Mama....just wait for it..."

Placing his hands over his ears, the man rocked back on his heels and closed his eyes, hoping to shut out the voices that taunted him. Seconds later, words echoing from across the street stopped his rocking. He opened his eyes, smiled, and watched as paramedics appeared in the doorway, pushing a loaded gurney out to the porch. Like ice melting in the spring sun, the tension inside him evaporated and the voices in his mind faded into white noise. Already the euphoric sensation that drove his need to watch filled him, replacing his pain. This was his high, and he craved it every bit as much as a street junkie craved the needle.

Running a hand through his dark, short-cropped hair, he watched the paramedics maneuver the gurney down three short steps to the sidewalk below. Sturdy green straps pulled tightly against the corpse, and held the black body bag in place. The wheeled death-cart interrupted the splay of cruiser lights on the side of the house, creating its own grim show of red and blue bouncing off the black plastic. They wouldn't need lights and sirens for this ride. Trips to the morgue were as silent as the bodies that were carried and stored there. He watched as the ambulance drove away with their still and silent passenger.

Saralyn Parker. Saralyn hadn't been so still hours before.

The memories were so fresh that he grew hard thinking about it. He'd entered the house moments after she'd stepped out of the shower. She'd stood head down toweling her long, sun-bleached blonde hair. He'd watched a good ten seconds before she'd raised her head and saw him, her mouth forming an "oh" of surprise.

Before she uttered a single word, he reached her, his fist cracking against her jaw sending the breath whooshing out of her lungs. He saw the pain twist her face as she dropped to her knees, a moan escaping her lips. Pushing her down to the bathroom floor, he pressed his body against her naked flesh. The warmth of her still wet skin seeped through his clothes. She fought...twisting, bucking, and turning in a futile attempt to loosen his grip. He watched as fear leached the color from her face, turning it a mask of ash grey. Sitting astride her, his erection strained against the fabric of his pants. As fear widened her big blue eyes, he smiled and pressed himself deeper against her taut abdomen. He leaned close so that his forehead rested against hers, then smiled and whispered, "Don't worry, it will be over soon. Much too soon."

And it was.

The man stood, stepped back, and stared at the lifeless body of Saralyn Parker as the blood drained from her body. A flowing river of red ran across her breasts where it dripped from one nipple to pool on a shaggy blue rug beneath her.

Squatting down to stare at the woman, he lifted his chin a notch, and with child-like defiance, chirped, "I didn't make a mess. I did it just like Daddy, and no one will ever know. You can't tell." Dropping his voice to a whisper, he continued, "Mama says that we can never tell...it's a secret."

The memory was crisp and fresh. Now, turning to leave his hiding spot in the shadows of the building, the man slid his hand into his jacket pocket, his fingers searched for the token he'd placed there when he'd left the house across the street hours before. He traced the etched design engraved on the coin, loving the feel of its surface and the power that it held.

CHAPTER 2

Tate Echo pulled his city-issued SUV into the courthouse parking lot, slipping the dark vehicle into the slot reserved for the Chief of Police. He parked and turned the engine off. Reaching over to the passenger seat for a well-worn Minnesota Twins baseball cap, he pushed his dark brown hair back with one hand, and slid the cap into place. He took a deep breath, preparing for the onslaught of questions he was sure to get this morning.

Already the local news station had a van onsite with a home-grown celebrity standing on the courthouse steps, waiting to questions him about last night's murder. Only problem was, he didn't have any answers. Not yet. Stepping out of the SUV, Tate made his way toward the gathering crowd, his long strides quickly eating up the pavement.

A thin and shaggy-haired cameraman made a sweep with his camera as the 'dressed for TV' anchorman stepped forward, attempting to block Tate's entry into the building. "Chief Echo, what can you tell us about the murder of Saralyn Parker? Any suspects yet? Where do you intend to focus your investigation?"

Tate sighed as the newscaster pushed the microphone toward him. He stopped and turned to face the camera, "No details can be released at this time. This is an open case, and the investigation is ongoing. My department is sharing details only on a need to know basis for now."

Not one to give up easily, the news anchor tried again, "Chief, can you confirm that Parker was sexually assaulted during the attack? Can you tell us...."

Turning away from the man, Tate took the courthouse steps two at a time, leaving the newsman behind, his words already fading.

"This is KCKY news anchor Wes Lively reporting on location at the Shannon County Courthouse..."

Reaching his office, Tate flipped on the overhead lights and started his small coffee maker. He moved to stare out a bank of windows on the north side of the room as he waited for the coffee to brew. The Black Hills of South Dakota rose up in the distance, their dark peaks matching his mood. As the coffee dripped, its strong rich smell permeated the room and Tate noticed that the crowd below was thinning, but there was still a group of ten or twelve locals who stood listening to Wes as he continued his broadcast. Grabbing a chipped stoneware mug that he'd pilfered from the courthouse cafeteria weeks ago, Tate filled it with the dark brew and walked to his desk and the mess that waited for him there in a closed manila folder. Glancing at his desk phone, Tate saw the blinking red voicemail light pulsing on the side, demanding his attention. With one push of the button he heard Gary Hooper, the mayor of Pine Ridge, leave his name and number demanding an immediate call back.

"Not yet, Mr. Mayor."

The next three messages were more of the same. The mayor again, followed by two city councilmen all wanting to know what he was doing to solve the tragic murder of Ms. Parker. Delete, delete, and delete.

"They must think they hired a damn psychic as police chief," he muttered.

Just as Tate opened the waiting Parker file, his cell phone rang. Snatching the phone from a brown leather holder clipped at his waist, he answered, "Echo here."

"Echo, this is Mayor Hooper. Tell me what's going on with the Parker case. Did you catch the killer yet?"

Tate pushed back his frustration and calmly explained, "The investigation is underway but it has been less than 24 hours. We'll have more to work with once we receive the ME's report."

Undeterred, the Mayor continued, "Echo, I know that you had some hot shot job with the FBI and was some kind of hero in the Marines, but I took a real chance hiring you as Chief. Hell, I worked my tail off to sway two councilmen to vote with me when they really wanted Chad Green in your seat. My damn phone hasn't stopped ringing with concerned citizens reaming me out about this murder and point out that I never should have hired you. For Christ's sake, Echo, this is an election year, and if you don't nail this son of a bitch, it's not going to look good for either of us. You do understand what I'm saying here, right?"

Tate pinched the bridge of his nose and struggled to tamp down his rising temper. He sucked in a deep breath and let it out slowly. Yeah, he understood a not so thinly veiled threat when he heard one. Politics. Damn he hated this part of the job. With a calmness that he didn't feel, Tate reassured the Mayor that he would solve this murder, promising to keep him better informed on the progress of the case.

Disconnecting the call, Tate wondered what really concerned the Mayor most, the murder of a sweet, local school teacher, or his upcoming run for re-election. It was bureaucratic crap like this-and if he were being honest with himself, a failed marriage-that prompted him to quit the bureau eight months ago and move back to his home town.

Having had too much from the job and too little from the marriage he'd packed up his truck and driven home to Pine Ridge, South Dakota, where he'd taken a job to serve and protect. *Great job protecting this one Echo*, he thought.

Flipping the manila case file open again, Tate stared at a digital print showing Saralyn Parker's naked and mutilated body lying in a bloody pool on her bathroom floor. Placing the photo on top of a stack of similar pictures and flipping the whole mess face down, Tate turned his attention to the report, pulling a neatly typewritten page from where it was paper clipped to the inside of the folder. Tate read, his mind absorbing details and compartmentalizing them into manageable bits and pieces. Finishing the written report, he pushed back from his desk and crossed his legs. He silently stared at the folder, willing it to talk.

"Every scene tells a story," he whispered. "What's yours Ms. Parker?" With a resigned sigh, he gave up on the folder's ability to verbalize a theory and slid his chair closer to the desk.

Tate turned over the previously ignored digital photos and spread them across his desk in order, based on the time stamp at the bottom of each one. Digital photos couldn't be used in court since they could easily be altered, but not wanting to wait for the crime team to develop and share their thirty five millimeter shots, Tate had instructed his team on site to also take the digitals.

Tate was still staring at the photos when his office door opened. He wasn't surprised to see Sheriff Martin Crawley. Nodding a greeting, Martin filled a cup with the last of the coffee before taking a seat across the desk from Tate. He leaned forward and scanned the photos covering the desk, then shuddered, "Good Lord man, what kind of sick bastard does this sort of thing?"

Looking up at the older man, Tate replied, "I don't know Martin, but I intend to find out. What I do know is that this was not some random burglary gone bad. This was a calculated kill. The bastard took his time and he made her hurt before he finished."

"You get the ME's report back yet?"

Tate shook his head. "Nothing yet. Crime team at the scene didn't find a damn thing. They ran the HEPA Vac and didn't pick up even one hair that didn't belong to Parker. No prints. Nothing. It was almost like the perp cleaned the place after the kill; if that's the case then the bastard did a good job. The preliminary confirms rape but techs found no body fluid or other DNA that we could use. I'm hoping that the Medical Examiner comes up with something that was missed on site. We could use a break here."

Nodding, Martin continued to sort through the photos on Tate's desk. After a moment he leaned back in his chair, "Tate, I know you were in the FBI and all, but I haven't ever seen anything like this in my eighteen years on the force here in Pine Ridge. Things have gone from bad to worse out at the Reservation in the last couple years, but nothing like this has happened out there either. You suppose she's got ties out at the Res?

Taking a sip from his cup, Tate considered the idea. "I don't know. Right now, I can only think that while it's not likely, it's certainly possible. I've been going through the photo sequence looking for anything that might be out of place, but nothing's jumping off the page at me, not yet anyway." Tate met the other man's eyes. "I wish I could say that this was just a rape and murder, but some of the cuts on her body push me to think otherwise."

Martin nodded his agreement and pointed to the photo nearest him, "I know what you mean, why would he cut her face up like that?" The photo in front of Martin showed Saralyn's face at close range, her eyes were closed, a three inch slash starting above her eyebrow cut diagonally down and across her right eye, ending at her cheek bone. Bulging from around the torn lid, a sliver of blue iris peaked out as if she were watching. In the corner of the shot lay an ear that had been surgically shaved off her head, and placed neatly on the bathroom rug. Once a shaggy blue, the blood-soaked rug appeared a matted purple in the photos.

"Seems very personal to me. Most often a rapist will kill the victim so that he can't be identified, but this type of mutilation and the level of overkill pints to another type of perp altogether." Tate continued, "It's like the damn 'see no evil, hear no evil' monkeys, except her tongue is still intact."

Martin picked up the next photo in the series, a full body shot showing Saralyn's nude form splayed across the bathroom floor, her hands bound with some type of red cording and a dark purple bruise on her left jaw. "I see that her hands were tied, but he'd still have to be a pretty big SOB to hold her still enough to make these cuts unless she was already dead when he cut her."

"I thought the same thing. The bruising on the left jaw suggests he slugged her at some point. Maybe she was unconscious when he finished the kill; otherwise he would have had to use something to subdue her in order to make cuts this precise. I do know that the kill was complete when he slashed her throat. Probably used a hunting knife or large kitchen knife to finish up. His own most probably, since there didn't appear to be any missing cutlery when we searched Parker's kitchen"

Martin placed the photo back on Tate's desk, "What about the red rope that he tied her hands with? That come from the house, or did he bring that too?"

Tate picked up the photo, and shrugged. "I'm not positive, but I think he brought it with him. It appears to be cording like you would use to tie back curtains, but there weren't any other pieces in the house and it doesn't match anything that we found. The medical examiner at the scene thinks, based on the blood pooling, that some of the cuts were definitely made while she was alive, but he really couldn't tell without further review. Same thing with the rape. We need that damn report. Either way, the cutting took time and skill. The bastard wasn't in any hurry, which means either he knew her or at the least he was familiar with her routine and not worried about being interrupted. Even if the mutilation cuts were made after he slashed her throat, it wouldn't have been quick."

Pointing to the last of the photos on Tate's desk, Martin asked, "What do you suppose this cut means? Looks like the Olympic rings, only there's three instead of five. Only someone who's really good with a knife could do that. It almost looks like a tattoo."

"I really don't know if there's any symbolic meaning. I have been doing some research online, but can't find anything that resembles that cut, other than the Olympic rings, and as you pointed out, that's not an exact match. Daniel Westhaven from the ME's office covered the scene and he wasn't familiar with any Native American symbols that bear any resemblance to the tattoo cut either."

Well if it is a Lakota symbol, then Daniel would know. He's pretty much an expert. Maybe she did have ties to the Reservation and this was some kind of drug deal gone bad." Martin pushed the prints back into the folder.

"Once we get the ME's report with a tox screen, we may have something more to go on with that line of thought."

Martin nodded. "Who found the body, Tate? God, I hope it wasn't her Mama or her Daddy."

"No one found the body, and that's the strangest piece in this whole grizzly puzzle. Julie Barton over at central dispatch got an anonymous 911 call from Parker's home phone. A male caller said he wanted to report a murder. The bastard actually laughed, then hung up before Julie could ask any questions."

Martin met Tate's eyes, stunned. "You've got to be shittin' me. The perp called in his own crime?"

Tate nodded. "Sounds crazy, I know, but that's what happened. When the assistant ME showed up, he put the time of death at approximately 7:30 pm. Hell, the body was still warm. Julie logged the call at 8:07 and immediately dispatched a patrol car to the house. When they got there, the door was standing open. The bastard must have called it in right after he killed her."

Whistling through his teeth, Martin shook his head, "Now that's a ballsy move. In all my years of service, I have never heard of the perp calling in his own crime."

Tate shrugged, "Why call it in at all? And why so fast? Why not buy himself some time by letting someone find the body after he was gone?"

Martin leaned back in his chair and pulled his glasses off, tucking them into his shirt pocket. "You ever get any calls out to her house before?"

"None," Tate shook his head. "No history of calls to the house, no husband at present or ex-husband, no known boyfriend and no clear ties to the Res. All I know for sure is that Saralyn Parker was a 24-year-old school teacher that some sick bastard raped, mutilated and killed."

Martin pushed his official sheriff's tan hat back on his head and stood to leave. "Any idea where you're going next with this investigation? Once this gets out, you're going to have your hands full with the locals. There hasn't been a murder in Pine Ridge for so long that once they move past the shock of it, they'll be out for blood. Yours if you don't come up with a suspect pretty quick."

Standing to shake Martin's hand, Tate said, "I know the locals expect a fast arrest, but we can't afford to be sloppy and lose a conviction on a technicality. I'm waiting on the report along with the tox screen, and hopefully it will give me some DNA evidence to work with. I've already had a call from the mayor reminding me that it's an election year, and letting me know how important it is to both of us to get this resolved."

"You mean he threatened your job?"

Tate offered a grim chuckle. "Well, not directly, but he did skip around it. Made sure he reminded me that he had to work his tail off to get me in over Chad Green."

Martin croaked, "'Green' being the operative word. Chad's just a kid, straight out of the academy. Just because his daddy's been on the County force forever doesn't mean that kid could run the department. You plan on having a press conference or something to let the locals know what's going on?"

"Not yet. Until we have some solid evidence, it's too early to be talking to the press or the locals. Right now, I plan to do some follow up with Reva Corley since she was the last person to see Parker alive. She said that they were hiking out at White's Lake earlier in the day. I talked to her last night and I can't be sure, but my gut tells me that she was holding something back. If that's true, I've got to find out whatever it is she's not telling me."

"Let me know when you get the ME's report back and if there's something I can do to help, just say the word."

"Thanks Martin, I will." Alone again, Tate dropped the Parker file into a desk drawer. He grabbed his cap and slipped out of the courthouse just behind Martin, avoiding as many curious people as possible.

CHAPTER 3

Tate slid into the hunter green SUV and pushed his sunglasses on, backed out of his reserved parking spot at the courthouse, and turned left on Main Street. With one hand he dialed the number for the Tribal Police on his cell only to learn that things were pretty quiet at the Reservation right now, if you didn't count the steady stream of drugs that continued to make their way onto tribal property. After a quick trip by the morgue where he was assured that the Parker case was getting priority, he made his way to the Ridge Diner, hoping that Reva Corley was working the day shift.

When he pushed open the glass door of the diner, a clanging cow bell overhead reminded Tate of just how little things in Pine Ridge had changed in the last couple of decades. The diner had been where all the kids hung out after school, including him. In front of the bar, the same round swivel stools sat atop dingy round chrome poles bolted to the floor, and even though there were older now, some of the same people still sat there, feet propped on an equally dingy chrome rail running the length of the bar. Nodding to those who turned to look his way, Tate moved to the back of the diner and slid into a faded red Naugahyde booth that matched the stools at the bar.

A petite woman with limp, blond hair stepped up to take his order. Her white shirt was covered with a dark brown apron sporting several grease spots and her sleeves were rolled up to the elbows. Smiling, she pulled a numbered pad from her pocket with one hand, and a pen from behind her ear with the other.

"What'll it be today Tate, uh, I mean Chief?" Kathy was the same age as Tate and they'd been in some classes together in high school. Looking up at her, Tate could see that life had been hard on the once beautiful girl.

Smiling as if he hadn't noticed the change at all, Tate ordered a club sandwich and a cup of coffee. Before Kathy could walk away, he asked, "Reva working today Kathy?"

Kathy shook her head. "She was just so upset over what happened to Saralyn and Burt gave her a couple days off. Told her to pull herself together and then come on back to work." As Kathy walked away, Tate leaned back into the worn booth, propping his feet up on the opposite seat. For the first time since he'd gotten called out to the Parker house, he relaxed.

The bell over the diner door clanked, and Tate watched as a tall man with long, graying hair pulled back in a tight ponytail entered the diner. Locking eyes with the man as he slid into the opposite side of the booth, Tate smiled.

"Hello, Son. I hear you're up to your nose in trouble these days."

Tate reached over and clasped his father's outstretched hand. "Yeah, Dad, I am. But you must be in some serious trouble too, if you're eating at the diner when we both know that you're married to the best cook in the state."

"Nothing like that, Son. You Mama just thought it was time I come to town to see about you. Claims she's not cooking a thing until I make sure our boy's alright." A frown creased the older man's forehead. "You are alright aren't you, Son?"

"I'm okay, but this case has got me thinking about things I haven't thought about since I left the bureau and moved back home—things like this just don't happen in Pine Ridge." Tate leaned forward and lowered his voice, "No leads and no obvious reason for the killing. Nothing seems to fit, at least not yet. This woman didn't seem to have an enemy in the world, yet someone went into her house and raped and killed her."

Jimmy Echo smiled at Kathy as she sat Tate's order down on the table, "Think about it some and it'll come to you. Might help if you let your hair grow a little longer!"

"I don't think the Mayor would understand it if I told him to put this case on the back burner while my hair grows long so that my spirit will be strong enough to catch a killer."

"You're probably right about that, but then people not understanding the Native ways has always been a problem for us. When your Unci, your grandmother, left the Reservation to marry your grandfather, folks in Pine Ridge thought he was crazy for getting tied up with an 'Indian' girl and people on the Res shunned my mother for leaving them for a white man. But that didn't stop them from building a good life together for over fifty years."

The two sat in silence as Tate ate his lunch.

Finally, Jimmy said, "Tate, I know you're busy, but at least call your Mama. She's worried sick about you. Says she's got a real bad feeling about all this and you know how she is when she gets a feeling about something." Rising to leave, Jimmy clasped a hand on his son's shoulder. "And Son, don't you worry none about this case, long hair or short, you'll figure it out."

Tate watched as his dad left the diner, stopping first to speak to several of the regulars perched on the round swivel seats at the bar.

Taking the last bite of his sandwich, Tate thought of the last time he'd seen his dad with short hair. It had been when his grandmother died. He was twelve and had followed his dad down to the creek behind their house. Silently he watched as his dad pulled his braid to the side and used a hunting knife to cut it off, and then knelt, placing it in the water before standing to watch it float away. It had been a few years later before Tate understood that his dad was honoring his Unci by grieving in the Native way, cutting his hair and returning it to the earth.

Tate dropped a generous tip on the table and rose to leave. Deciding to give Reva a day's reprieve before answering questions, he drove to Saralyn Parker's house, hoping to find something that had been overlooked the night before. An hour later, he admitted to himself that it had been a long shot and a dry run. Tate locked the small house, stepped over the yellow crime scene tape and made his way back to his SUV.

On the drive home he made a mental note to call his mom. Tate's parents were first rate, family was everything to them. His dad owned the only garage in town and was the best mechanic in the county. Karlee wasn't his real mother, but she was the only mother he'd ever remembered or needed. She'd always loved him and made sure that he knew it.

On the short ride to his house, Tate let his thoughts drift to his parents and to his real mother. Jimmy Echo had married a young local girl shortly after high school; rumor was that she had been pregnant and 'that Echo boy had done right by her'. Six months after Tate was born, she'd left. His dad claimed he came home from work one day and knew something was wrong when he pulled his wrecker into the drive. Said he heard Tate crying from the moment he opened the truck door. He'd gone inside and found Tate in his crib, soaked and hungry. There was no sign of his young wife other than a note saying that she 'couldn't take no crying baby no more'. As far as Tate knew, she never came back. Never called to check on him, never cared.

"Not one damn birthday card," he muttered. His dad always laughs when he tells the story, though Tate suspected that it wasn't very funny at the time. Jimmy had picked up a crying Tate that night; changed his first diaper, and never looked back. Seven months later, he married Karlee. They'd tried to have children but after a couple miscarriages, Karlee gave up, saying that she had a beautiful son and that was what was most important to her.

That's the kind of marriage Tate had wanted when he'd married FBI Agent Emma Gage. Em was beautiful, smart, sexy as hell and he'd loved her on sight...who was he kidding? He still loved her. The marriage had lasted three years before things unraveled. Tate wanted kids and a job that got him home every night, but Emma had a career path that didn't include taking time off for pregnancy or raising a family. Eventually, they'd realized that while their dreams could come true, they wouldn't be together.

Pulling into his drive, Tate shook off thoughts of the past, checked his mail, and made his way into the small two bedroom house that he'd bought when he'd returned to Pine Ridge. He rummaged in the frig for a beer, and flipped on the TV. Tate wasn't surprised to see a local news station talking about the Parker case. This time the talking head was on remote and stood in front of Parker's mailbox, the yellow crime tape surrounding the small house in the background. A photo of Saralyn sat in the corner of the screen smiling as she posed with her elementary class. Reaching for the remote, Tate quickly changed the channel.

CHAPTER 4

The following morning, Daniel Westhaven, the Assistant Medical Examiner of Shannon County, dropped the ME's official report on Tate's desk. "Not much more here than we already knew, Tate. Royce did find seminal fluid on the exam, but the sample proved to be pre-ejaculate in nature. No sperm released."

Holding his hand up, Tate interrupted Daniel. "So you're saying he didn't find release during the rape?"

Daniel nodded, "Exactly. He didn't finish what he started. Either he couldn't, or maybe he got interrupted. Royce sent the results to the State DNA Databank for processing and entry into CODIS just this morning."

Tate glanced from the report to Daniel, "With any luck, we'll get a match. Don't suppose you know what the backlog is over there? I know it usually takes ten days for entry into the system, be we need answers now."

"No idea on the backlog, but Royce did tag it as priority which should bump it to the front of the line for you. Another interesting finding showed up in the toxicology report which really surprised the hell out of me. Seems that Ms. Parker might have a thing for drugs."

Reaching for the report, Tate slipped it from the letter sized manila envelope as Daniel continued. "We found a trace amount of marijuana along with Ketamine."

Tate glanced up from the report. "Ketamine? That drug was recently linked to a case of date rape and made national news."

Daniel nodded, "Yeah, it's usually used by vets and hospitals for anesthesia, but there's a big street market for it as well. Kids call it 'Special K'."

Tate closed the report and gave Daniel his full attention. "So save me some research and tell me everything you know about Ketamine."

"Well, Ketamine Hydrochloride, or 'Special K', can be injected, snorted, or swallowed." Daniel took a seat across from Tate. "It can take from less than a minute or up to five minutes to take full effect, depending on how it was taken and the amount. We did find a small puncture wound on Parker and think that she most likely injected the drug. It stays in the blood for a few hours depending on the dose size, but the effects on a casual user generally wear off in an hour or so. With the concentration ration that she tested, Royce thinks that she must have taken it right before she was murdered. Sounds like she was having a little K party that went wrong."

Royce Wiggins was in his mid-sixties and had served Shannon County as Senior Medical Examiner for more than three decades. Daniel Westhaven had signed on as the Assistant ME about four years ago when age and arthritis forced Royce to slow down and lighten his workload.

Daniel was in his late thirties and he took responsibility for most of the field work, leaving Royce to handle the in-house examinations and much of the paperwork that came with being the County Coroner. It was a given that Daniel would step into Royce's shoes once the old man retired.

Pushing back from his desk, Tate thought aloud, "Maybe she didn't give herself the injection. Maybe the killer gave it to her just before she was murdered. From what I recall in the news report, they said that Ketamine creates a trance-like state that significantly impairs motor function."

"That's true. Users call it the 'K-hole' when they get a floating out of body experience. Says it makes them feel paralyzed."

"Daniel, I'm still going to follow up on possible drug abuse by Parker, but I think it's more likely that the killer used Ketamine to subdue her. Would you agree that if the killer used it, that it's possible she was awake but unable to move when he raped and killed her?"

"Hell of a way to go," Daniel said. "If your assumptions are right, then she probably watched while he cut on her. Royce did confirm that the smaller cuts, eye, ear and those on her arm were not what killed her and that they were made while she was still alive."

"He would have had to subdue her in order to make cuts that exact. I already expected you would find something in her tox screen, I just wasn't sure what it would be." Tate frowned, "So what happens if he gives his victim too much?"

Daniel shrugged, "Well, most likely it would have stopped her breathing, since a true overdose would paralyze the organs, including the lungs, but since Royce confirmed that she was alive when the cuts were made, we know that didn't happen. Ketamine increases blood pressure and heart rate, so it might impact an unhealthy or elderly person differently than it would a young and otherwise healthy user."

"So he's educated on administering Ketamine, giving her enough to immobilize her but not kill her, and he's skilled with a knife. Now the marijuana use puts a bit of a spin on things." Tate's voice did nothing to hide his frustration. "You say it was just a trace amount?"

"Yeah, she could have smoked any time in the last thirty days and we'd have pulled a trace reading on the report."

Tate sighed, "Well, this just gets worse by the minute. Unless she was taking something legal that created a false positive on the marijuana, then it's possible that she was both a pot smoker and abused the Ketamine. Or maybe the killer injected her, and then forced her to smoke the week. Ask Royce to do a hair follicle at a ninety day and full year interval. That should tell us if she was a regular smoker or not."

Tate slid the report pages into the case file and flipped the folder closed. "Thanks for bringing the report over, Daniel. I appreciate that you guys down at the ME's office understand just how sensitive this is. We haven't had a murder in Pine Ridge in so long that folks are shocked and running scared."

"It just doesn't seem right that an elementary school teacher would be on drugs." Daniel said. "Hell, I've got little ones that will be starting school next year. I hate to think that we might be sending our kids off to spend the day with a user."

"The world is a scary place. I know that the school system does random drug tests on all the staff, so if she were a regular user then she probably would have lost her job before now. Hell, maybe she was a casual smoker. Guess I'll go back to her house and check to see what she's got there, even though we've had two empty searches already. I can't rule out drugs being part of the motive now and if they are, it points a strong finger toward the Reservation since that's where we have the biggest population of users in the state."

Daniel nodded, "You do know that while there is certainly a marijuana problem at the Res, more of the users there are into crack cocaine, right? I pull shifts over at County Hospital twice a month and there's always someone being brought in with a suspected overdose. A couple weeks ago, we had one show up and confirmed an OD on heroin. Surprised the hell out of me since I didn't know that there was enough money on the Res for anyone to get their hands on anything other than the cheap drugs, like marijuana or crack."

"Yeah, I knew that there were other drugs out there. Rumor has it that the gangs are pulling down some big money delivering for their primary supplier, and we both know that for an addict, more money equals better drugs. Any idea what Ketamine goes for on the street?"

Snorting, Daniel replied, "No idea. That's more your department than mine."

"Just a casual question, Daniel. You find anything more on that symbol she had cut into her arm? Maybe it's Lakota after all?"

"If I were guessing, I'd say it's not a Native American symbol, Lakota or otherwise. You thinking someone from the Res did this?"

Tate shrugged, "Just thinking outside the box. I need to understand what the symbol means and why the perp would mark the victim this way. I haven't ruled out that the guy wants us to think that the killer is someone from the Reservation. I'm not aware of any murders, on or off the Res where the killer marked the victim this way, but I don't want to overlook anything either."

Daniel stood to leave and Tate extended his hand. "I appreciate you help. If you think of anything else just give me a call, and keep an eye out for any Ketamine cases over at County when you're pulling shifts, if you would."

"No problem. In fact, I can do you one better and check the hospital systems for any reported Ketamine cases. I'm on duty over there this weekend and I'll let you know if I come up with anything. Once Royce has results on the hair follicle findings, I'll give you a call."

Tate grabbed his cap and slid his Glock G22 service revolver into the black leather holster at his waist. Tate walked with Daniel as far as the parking lot. Climbing into his SUV, he decided it was time to drive out and visit with Reva Corley whether she'd gotten herself together or now. He needed the truth about Saralyn Parker's drug use, and starting with her best friend seemed as good a place as any.

CHAPTER 5

Turning onto County Road 42, Tate followed the winding two lane road out to Miller's Haven trailer park, where Reva Corley lived. Once into the mobile home community, Tate immediately noticed signs of neglect. The entrance was marked by rough-hewed timbers on either side of the road leading into the park. Handing on one side of the timbers, a dangling piece of rusty chain held a faded wooden sign proclaiming the place as a 'Haven', while on the other side, an equally rusty mate sporting the name 'Miller's', swung in the afternoon breeze.

"Not much of a haven," he muttered.

Faded trailers sat on gray cinder blocks or on the wheels that they were sold with, and were separated by thirty feet of overgrown grass, dirt and rock. Tate smiled when he saw that several dogs had taken a break from the spring sun and snoozed in the shade of the homes that weren't underpinned. Pulling into the driveway on lot thirty eight, Tate noticed that Reva's home wasn't in much better shape than the others, but that she did keep it neat. The area around her trailer had been mowed and on both sides of the steps leading up to her door she'd placed planters that bloomed with red and yellow spring flowers. Flowers that reminded him of the window boxes at Saralyn Parker's neat little one-story house in town.

Stepping up to the door, Tate heard a radio blasting rock music and caught the greasy scent of something being fried. He knocked and stepped back a few feet to wait. No answer. After a few minutes, he knocked again, and heard the scrape of a metal chain sliding from its lock. The door opened a crack, just wide enough for Reva to see outside.

"Oh, it's you. Come on in." Reva pulled the door open and stepped back, motioning him inside.

Tate stepped into a small rectangular living room, and glanced at Reva; her green eyes were dark-rimmed and red against the ash-white color of her bare face. Her strawberry blonde hair was pulled back in a ponytail, making her appear much younger than her twenty-four years. In one hand she held a pot holder, and in the other, a metal spatula dripping with oil.

"Come on in the kitchen and have a seat. I'm almost done here." Stepping around a worn dining room table that had probably belonged to her mother before her, Reva moved to the stove and the black cast iron skillet that sat bubbling on one burner. She reached into the cabinet and pulled down a glass bowl to scoop the frying potatoes out of the grease-coated skillet. Once the task was complete, Reva turned the stove's gas burner off and set the bowl on the counter. She looked at Tate, a sad smile on her face. "Have you found out who killed Saralyn? Is that what you came to tell me?"

Tate laid his cap on the yellow Formica table and sat in one of the chairs. "No, we haven't caught the killer yet, but I do have a couple questions for you about Saralyn." A deep sigh pushed from his lungs, "Were you aware that she smoked marijuana, Reva?" Tate didn't mention the Ketamine.

Lunch forgotten, Reva stood behind a chair at the table across from Tate. Gripping the back of the chair until her knuckles turned white, she leaned forward, her green eyes sparking with anger. "Saralyn was *not* a dope user. She may have taken a toke every now and then, but that's it."

Not breaking eye contact with her, Tate's voice was soft and firm. "What do you mean every now and then, Reva? Did she smoke every day, once a week, how often *is* every now and then?" Tate watched as Reva sucked in a deep breath and let it out slowly, he continued to press her for answers. "Where'd she get it? She have connections out at the Res, or was it brought in from somewhere else?"

Reva pulled the chair in front of her out, and dropped into the seat. She cupped her chin with both hands and raised her watery eyes, meeting Tate's gaze with her own. "Get this Tate Echo. Saralyn was not a drug user. As far as I know she only smoked once since she graduated college and moved back to Pine Ridge to teach. She told me that she went to a party at her cousin's house over in White River a couple weeks ago where she met a guy and they really seemed to click. They stepped out on the porch to talk and he pulled out a joint. She took a few tokes. Nothing more."

Tate leaned forward and met Reva's gaze, "She mention any other drugs to you?"

"Other drugs? No, why would she? There weren't any."

Ignoring her question, Tate continued to pepper Reva with questions of his own. "Who's the guy, did she tell you that? I need to talk to him. Maybe he had something to do with her death."

Tears pooled in Reva's eyes and spilled down her cheeks to the corner of her mouth. Hesitantly, she said, "His name was Troy. Saralyn didn't tell me a last name. Tate, she didn't see him again after that. Saralyn wanted to fall in love and have kids, and she knew she couldn't do that with a drug user, not ever a casual user." Pulling a paper napkin from a ceramic U-shaped holder on the table, Reva dabbed at her eyes then folded the napkin and blew her nose before wadding it in one hand.

"Me and Saralyn were friends since grade school, and I know that she was telling me the truth. If there'd been more to tell, then I'd know about it. We loved each other like sisters, and we did *not* keep secrets. For God's sake Tate, her daddy is a deacon at the Baptist church and her mama teaches Sunday school. It would kill them to find out that Saralyn smoked weed, even if it was only once. Please, you can't let this get out."

Tate leaned back in the chair and crossed his arms. "I have no intention of letting anything get out, but I do need to track down this guy. Do you know her cousin's name? Maybe he can fill me in about Troy."

Reva nodded. "We both know him. It's Danny Parker. He was two grades ahead of me and Saralyn. He works over at the feed store in White River now. He does deliveries for them."

With a nod signaling that their conversation was over, Tate stood, grabbed his cap from the table and turned to leave.

Standing when Tate did, Reva whispered, "Is it true that Saralyn was cut up?"

Spinning to face her, Tate swore under his breath. "Reva, where did you hear that?"

Unable to meet Tate's cold grey eyes, Reva ducked her head. "I only asked about it, because if it's true...well, I thought you should know that there's only one man in the county mean enough, and good enough with a knife to do something like that."

Relaxing his posture slightly, Tate waited for her to continue. "Go on."

Glancing up, Reva knew that she had Tate's attention. "Marshall Olen is always flashing that knife of his and bragging about cutting somebody if they don't do what he says. I just thought you should know that. He eats over at the diner real regular and I...well, I overhear things sometimes."

"Reva, I appreciate you sharing what you know about Marshall, and I will follow up on where he was the night Saralyn died. For now, I don't want you to repeat any of what you just told me to anyone. I mean it, no one. Talking that way could put you in danger and I know that neither of us wants that. I'll need your word."

Reva's eyes widened, realizing what Tate meant. "Oh God Tate, you think that if he killed Saralyn that he might come after me too?" Her voice was little more than a whisper. "I never even thought of that. I won't say a word. Not one word. I swear to you, I swear it."

"That's good. Now if you think of anything else, or happen to overhear anything else suspicious in the diner, you keep quiet about it and then you give me a call. For Christ's sake, and especially for your own safety, do not talk to anyone about the details of Saralyn's murder. You can't trust what you might overhear at the diner and repeating it just fuels the fire for speculation. You understand?"

Nervously rubbing her hands together, Reva nodded. "I do understand and I just want you to catch the person who killed Saralyn. She deserves that."

Tate slammed his cap down on his head. "I intend to catch the killer, but this is an open investigation and my office hasn't released any of the particulars about Saralyn's murder. Obviously someone on the scene has a big mouth. We need to keep this as quiet as possible so that it doesn't interfere with the investigation or with finding the bastard who did this."

Reva nodded a frightened 'yes', and stood silent as Tate took the steps two at a time and jogged to his SUV.

Five minutes later, Tate passed under the rusted and dangling sign as he left Millers Haven. At least now he had a lead. Make that two leads and a possible suspect. That was more than he'd had since Saralyn's body had been found. At this point, Tate agreed with Reva that there was no need to disclose the drugs found during the autopsy to Saralyn's parents. Not until he knew more about how they got into her system. The Parker family had been through enough losing their child without finding out that she was a pot smoker and possibly more.

Instead of turning his SUV west toward town and his office, Tate turned east toward White River. *Might as well go on over and find out if Danny Parker can give me more details on this Troy guy, then do a little digging to see what Marshall Olen was up to the night that Saralyn was murdered.* Tate called dispatch with instructions to forward all his calls to his cell.

On the drive to White River, he thought about Reva's comments on Marshall Olen. Punching Martin's number in his cell he waited for him to answer.

"Crawley here. That you Tate?"

"Yeah Martin, it's me. Wondering if you can do me a favor and see if you can find out what Marshall Olen was up to the night Parker was murdered."

"I got that. You thinking Marsh had something to do with this mess?"

Clearing his throat, Tate replied, "Don't know, but when I talked to Reva she seemed to think that he brags a lot about what he's going to do with that knife of his. I've only seen Marsh once since I returned to Pine Ridge and that was when

I ran back up for you out at the I-31 Tavern and by the time I got there the fight was over. You remember that night?"

Sure do. Never could prove who started the fight or that Marsh was the one who cut Jack Long's arm up, even though I suspect he was."

Flipping his blinker on, Tate grimaced. "Yeah, that's what I thought too. He's a big SOB, and on top of that, he's a mean drunk and a bully. When you were questioning folks, I watched him sitting at the bar. He followed you in the mirror the whole time. I remember thinking that he acted suspicious, but when no one in the tavern wanted to tell you what happened, I figured it would have been a waste of time to pull him in with no witnesses to support a case."

"You're right about that. No need to waste the taxpayer's money on a bar room fight if you don't have a credible witness. I'll check up on Marshall's whereabouts the night of the murder and let you know what I find out."

"Sounds good. Stop by my place on your way home tonight and I'll have you a cold beer ready. I'm headed over to White River to follow up on a lead there and expect to be home about six."

Twenty minutes later, Tate pulled into the parking lot of the White River Feed and Supply. Tate stepped out of the SUV just as Danny Parker walked out on the loading dock with a sack of feed resting on one shoulder. Leaning against the front of the vehicle, Tate waited while Danny dropped the bag into the bed of an old truck and waved at the man driving it. As the truck pulled away from the dock, Tate walked to where Danny stood.

"You got a minute Danny?"

Jumping from the dock, Danny extended a hand to Tate. "Haven't seen you in a while, Tate. I heard you were the new police chief in Pine Ridge, but I don't get over there much. What can I do for you?"

"I've got a couple questions for you about Saralyn. I know that she was at a party at your place a few weeks ago and that she hung out with a guy named Troy. I need his last name and where I can find him."

Whistling through his teeth Danny didn't hesitate, "Donaldson, Troy Donaldson. You thinking that he had something to do with Saralyn's murder?

Tate leaned against the dock, "I'm not saying that, Danny. I just have a few questions for him. You have any idea where I might find him?"

"He lives in the duplexes over on Center Street. He's in the second unit on the right, middle door. He travels a lot for work and I don't know if he's in town right now."

"Did you notice Saralyn hanging out with anyone else in particular at the party?" Tate straightened.

"No, not really. Her and Troy kind of hit it off right away and they pretty much hung out together the whole night. I didn't spend the night keeping a close eye on my little cuz or anything, but I didn't see her dancing with anyone else or even talking to anyone else for more than a minute."

"Fair enough. I may have some more questions for you later, but I think that about covers it for now."

A few minutes later, Tate turned on Center Street and pulled in at the driveway of the second duplex unit, parking behind a blue sedan.

Tate knocked on the door and stepped back. A man in his late twenties opened the door a few seconds later. Looking surprised, the man asked, "Yes, can I help you?"

"Are you Troy Donaldson?"

Troy nodded and stepped out of the house, pulling the door almost closed behind him. "I'm Troy Donaldson."

Tate pulled his jacket back to reveal the badge clipped at his waist. "I'm Police Chief Tate Echo from Pine Ridge and I have some questions for you regarding the murder of Saralyn Parker."

Troy shot a nervous glance around to see if any neighbors were watching, and then pushed the door behind him open. "Come on in. I don't think I want to talk about Saralyn standing on my front stoop."

Walking into the small duplex, Tate was surprised to see that it was well care for and clean. *Not what you'd expect from a junkie.*

Troy pointed to the couch, "Have a seat. Can I get you something to drink? I have bottled water and soft drinks."

Ignoring the offer, Tate got to the point. "Can you tell me where you were the night that Saralyn Parker was murdered?"

Troy dropped into a chair across from Tate. "I was in Milwaukee on business. I do sales for Spartan Electronics and I travel a lot."

Holding the younger man's gaze, Tate asked, "You ever do Ketamine? Or maybe you know it as Special K?"

Sliding forward in the chair, Troy stared at Tate. "I know what it is, but I haven't ever done it. I thought we were going to talk about Saralyn. What's Ketamine got to do with her?"

Tate cleared his throat. "I know that you and Saralyn smoked pot at a party over at Danny Parker's house and I want to know if you and she did any other drugs."

Jumping to his feet, Troy paced before turning back to

Tate. "I smoke a little weed every now and then, but I don't do any other drugs. Saralyn only took a couple tokes from a joint that I carried to Danny's party and nothing else. Hell, I'd be willing to take a drug test if that would help you out." Dropping back into his chair, Troy spoke softly. "We talked almost the whole night and I thought we hit it off pretty well. But she never returned my call, so I let it go. You know, thought she wasn't interested after all."

Cocking his head, Tate thought that either this kid was being totally honest or he was one hell of a good actor. "You have anyone that can verify you were in Milwaukee?"

"Absolutely." Troy pulled a business card out of his wallet and handed it to Tate. "That's my manager; he was at the same sales even and can confirm that I was there."

Standing, Tate extended a hand to Troy. "I appreciate you talking to me and I will be contacting your manager for confirmation. I could have some additional questions later, but I think that about covers it for now."

Backing out of the driveway, Tate pulled the business card that Troy had given him out of his shirt pocket and dialed the number. A very brief conversation confirmed what Tate had already suspected, Troy was telling the truth about being in Milwaukee. Another dead end.

CHAPTER 6

Hours later, Tate and Martin sat on the raised wooden deck behind Tate's house, each nursing their second beer of the evening.

"It's too bad that you lead with that guy from White River didn't pan out," Martin said. "Any idea where you're taking the investigation next?"

Tate took a pull from his bottle. "I'm not sure where I'll go from here," he admitted. "but wherever it is, I'd better do it soon. I did some follow up at Parker's house and didn't find anything that would indicate heavy drug use, and the story that I got from Troy Donaldson checks out. Basically he told me the same thing that Reva did and his employer verified that he was in Milwaukee the night Saralyn was murdered."

Raising his own bottle to his lips, Martin stopped and asked, "You ask him about Ketamine?"

"Absolutely. He swears he's never done Ketamine and even offered to do a drug test for me. That really doesn't mean much since K only stays in the system a couple days, and he'd probably test clean. My gut tells me that he's being honest." Settling his bottle back on the table, Tate continued, "Troy readily admitted that he's a casual smoker and that while he thought he and Saralyn hit it off pretty well, that she never returned his call after the party. He has a squeaky clean record and holds down a full time job. When I got back from White River, I did go ahead and check Saralyn's phone records from the night of the party forward and that part of his story is solid too. On the day she was killed there were only a couple of calls on record. She got an early morning call from Reva and nothing else in or out until the 911 call was made that night. I should get the hair follicle results from Royce or Daniel tomorrow and that will confirm if this really was a one-time thing or if there's a history of marijuana use."

Martin leaned back in his chair and crossed his legs, "Well, Marsh sure has a solid alibi. Four days in the Rushville lock up pretty much clears him on this one. Maybe someone who saw Saralyn and Reva out at the lake that day followed her into town."

"I've thought of that too, and I did question Reva about it but she says that she doesn't recall seeing anyone who seemed out of place. Says they didn't talk to anyone other than the clerk at the sign in desk. When I checked the records for that day there were twelve people, including Parker and Reva, who registered on the west side of the lake. I was able to interview them all in person with the exception of one couple who had driven over from Nebraska for the weekend, and I talked to them on the phone. I got pretty much the same story from them all, quiet day at the lake, good day for fishing and so on."

Martin tossed his empty bottle in a trash basket near the door, where it clinked against the other bottles already deposited there. "Of course we both know that not everyone who visits the lake takes the time to sign in or even coves into the park from the posted entrances." He stood, "I've got to be going Tate, I'm pretty sure Barb has my supper waiting and as good as that woman is to me, I try not to make her wait."

"I hear you, Martin," Tate said. "If I had a woman like Barb waiting for me, I'd be rushing to get home every day. I'll see you at the courthouse tomorrow."

CHAPTER 7

Ten miles away at the White Clay Lodge and Lake Resort, Gavin Wheeler stood before a full length mirror hanging on the bathroom door of the small cabin he'd rented earlier in the week. Critically looking at his image, he reached up and smoothed his thin mustache down against his upper lip. Satisfied that he looked like the average tourist out for a hike around the lake, he pushed his sunglasses down and winked at his reflection.

"Gavin, you are one good looking SOB. Johnny Depp doesn't have a thing on you." Grabbing his Steelers cap from the bed and settling it over his dark brown hair, he reached back to finger comb the short hair at the back of his neck. He snatched his backpack from the sofa and pulled out a small hand-held GPS. Once out the door, Gavin took the nearest hiking trail circling White Clay Lake.

The well-marked trails running through the park were covered with a thick layer of pine needles that both cushioned and muted his steps. Gavin followed the GPS directions using the coordinates that he had entered before leaving the cabin. The mid-day sun peaked through the trees, shading the tail and tossing shadows as a breeze rocked the limbs overhead. The sweet, piney smell of the trees reminded Gavin of home, and of his mother. He stopped and pulled a water bottle from his backpack, and looked out over the glass-like surface of the lake. Even though the summer season was still a couple weeks away, the lake was dotted with small boats of fisherman and families out for some fun.

Glancing back at the GPS, Gavin saw that he was almost at the cache site. Picking up his pace, he continued to follow the trail around the lake. A steady beeping signaled that he had reached the cache and prompted him to step off the trail. Pushing through a thick copse of undergrowth and vines, he followed the on screen display until the machine spoke.

"You have reached your destination," an automated voice said.

He turned the device off and slid it into his backpack. Gavin knew that he was as close to the geocache as the GPS could get him. Now he would have to search for the cache using the clues that were given as a hint on the geocaching website. Standing in a small clearing surrounded by pine and cedar trees, Gavin stopped to scan the area looking for a good place to hide something small. Pulling a pair of thin cotton gloves from his jacket pocket, he slipped them on, and stepped around a clump of brushy growth. Gavin bent to check under the ledge of a rock shelf near the edge of the clearing.

"Elementary, my dear Watson. Amateurs always hide it under the rocks."

Opening the small square plastic container wrapped in brown and green camouflage tape, Gavin wasn't surprised to see that it held several small trinkets. "The usual stuff," he muttered as he looked through the items in the cache.

Pushing aside a mini deck of playing cards, a small wooden cross that looked like it belonged on a keychain, and a toy car whose red paint had faded and chipped with wear, he saw that folded at the bottom of the container was a log book. "Not happening, fellow cachers."He didn't sign log books and he didn't take trinkets, but he would be leaving something of great personal value for the next cacher to find.

Gavin reached into his pocket and pulled out the coin. He took a minute to gently rub his finger along the etched design on the coin's surface. Three interlocking rings rose slightly from the otherwise smooth surface of the coin. Flipping the token in his palm, he did the same with the custom design on the other side. Block lettering proclaimed, 'Let the Chase Begin'. He smiled, "You're *not* just unusual, you *are* extraordinary."

Not much bigger than a fifty cent piece, the token was an eye catcher. Cachers couldn't resist taking the token, and Gavin couldn't resist killing them when they did. Rubbing the coin with the tips of his fingers had become a ritual that the coin required and Gavin never disappointed the coin. Closing his eyes and breathing deeply, Gavin could almost smell the dime store gardenia perfume that his mother had always worn. He could see her smiling face as she pushed his unruly hair from his forehead and bent to kiss his brow. The coin would give him the strength to do what had to be done, it always had.

"Don't worry Mama, it won't take long," he whispered. Gavin gently placed the token inside the plastic container and returned the cache to its hiding place, making sure to push the leaves around the rocks so that the site appeared undisturbed. "Don't want any 'muggles' finding this one do we Mama? Funny word 'muggles', huh, Mama? I think the cachers stole it from a Harry Potter book or movie. Anyway, we don't want any 'muggles' jacking this site. If they do, then I sincerely hope they can't resist taking our coin."

He stepped back to look at the site and once he was satisfied that the cache was well hidden, Gavin made his way over to a tall pine tree some fifteen feet away. Nimbly grabbing onto a lower limb and pulling up, he hoisted his body up into the tree. Sitting with his legs wrapped around the tree limb, Gavin pulled open his backpack and removed a small, motion activated camera, and secured it near the end of the tree limb. "I didn't get to record that bitch Saralyn, but I'm not going to miss another one," he grunted.

Gavin wrapped the camera tightly to the limb with brown duct tape and pushed a small battery pack into the waiting slot. He bent down to look over the unit making sure that his view to the cache site was clear. "Perfect, Gav. Won't be long and you'll have another video to add to your collection." He shimmied down the tree and pushed his backpack into place, then walked over to the rocks that hid the cache. He looked up, smiled at the camera, and waved. He sat on the rocks and pulled his water bottle free, taking a long draw of tepid water and a deep breath. Pushing his sunglasses up, Gavin looked around the site, noting that the trailhead was a good forty feet from the cache site.

"This is a good one Gav, just far enough to provide a little privacy."

Leaning back on the rocks, he closed his eyes, letting the morning sun warm him as his mind wandered. Placing the camera always reminded him of his daddy, the bastard. Harold Wheeler had owned a small gun and taxidermy shop when Gavin was a kid, and he'd used game cameras to photograph sites where he would later return to hunt deer. Hell, Gavin had used a game camera himself, back when still shots were enough...before fate had become his God, the coin his destiny. He whispered, "This is so much better *Daddy*. No grainy still shots for me, and once I do the remote disconnect, I'm done." Daddy—just saying the word choked him.

Before Gavin could stop them, memories of another day in the woods pushed at him, insisting that he open his mind's door and let them in. He'd been nine years old and his Daddy was letting him go on the hunt. They'd left the house in a battered old farm truck with rusted floorboards. It was early fall and still hot. The truck didn't have air condition and they'd rolled the windows down, dust circled in the cab as they bumped down a dirt logging road. Later, they'd sat in that damn tree stand for hours waiting for a deer to show up. He'd begged to climb down and pee but his daddy had only slapped him on the head.

Gavin could still hear the old man's voice. "Shut up boy, you can't be pissin' out here. Once a deer catches wind of human piss they won't come within a mile of this place. I knowed I should've left you home 'cause you ain't nothing but a sissy ass kid. Got your Mama to thank for that."

Gavin remembered shrinking down in the stand, crossing his legs and rocking himself, willing his body to hold on. He could still hear the rifle shot as it echoed in the small space, the scent of gunpowder filling his nose, the spent casing popping from the gun to land on the rough and faded wood floor of the stand. "Come on boy, I got one." Harold Wheeler had lifted him by the arms and dropped him to the ground. Gavin had watched the deer as it thrashed and struggled to stand while blood streamed from a hole in its chest. Fear kept him rooted to the spot, his eyes glued on the downed animal whose body was unmarked except for the single bullet hole piercing its heaving chest. Harold walked quickly over to the deer, placed his gun on its head and pulled the trigger, blowing half the animal's head away with the shot.

"Damn ugly animal, didn't have a rack worth trying to save the head for." Then the old man shot him a yellow-toothed smile and handed him a knife, "Well, boy, I killed it and that means that you gotta clean it."

Goosebumps pricked his arms as Gavin recalled how afraid he'd been. Not just of what he was being told to do, but of what would happen if he didn't do it right. His hands shook as he made a long sweeping cut across the deer's neck just like his daddy told him to do. Squeezing his closed eyes tighter he remembered the metallic smell of the animal's blood as it poured out and pooled at his feet. He still felt his old man's hand on his back, pushing him forward. He saw himself as he fell to his knees and the animal's crimson blood soaked through his jeans.

Gavin jumped up from his seat on the rocks and stumbled toward the trees. Almost there, he stopped. Standing alone in the woods, he shook his head, willing the memories away. It didn't work. There he was, a skinny nine year old with his hands braced against a pine tree, puking his guts up while urine ran down his legs and soaked into his jeans. It mixed with the animal's blood to form red trails down his pants legs. What was his old man doing? Laughing. Even now, he could still hear the SOB laughing.

"Bastard. You sorry bastard! I hated you just a little bit more every time you told that fucking story to your friends, and I hate you today. Well, guess what old man? You'd be the one pissing his pants if you could see me hunting now."

Retracing his steps to the edge of the clearing, Gavin was startled when a group of people broke through a patch of brush and stepped into the clearing just a few feet from him. Damn, he'd been so caught up in his own thoughts that he hadn't even heard them coming. Even worse, it was a family. The man held a GPS, just like his own, in one hand while the other hand was locked with a dark-haired woman's hand. Bringing up the rear there were two boys, maybe eight and ten. Both sported baseball caps and small school-sized backpacks.

The woman looked up at him, smiled and asked, "So, did you fine it?" Pushing forward, the smaller boy moved behind the man, using his father as a shield.

Gavin cleared his throat and turned to face the family, "Un, no, I didn't find the cache. My batteries just died and I forgot to bring a spare set." Stepping around the group he pulled his cap lower and again turned toward the trail. He'd only taken a few steps when the older boy called out.

"Hey mister, you can look with us if you want to.'

Then the younger one poked his head from around his father and added, "Yeah, we always find 'em. My dad's the best at finding caches."

Turning part way to face the man, Gavin smiled, "Uh, maybe some other time. I really do have to be going. Hope you find it." He really did hope they'd find it, in fact you might say that he needed them to find it.

CHAPTER 8

Tate watched from his office window as the sun dipped low and fell behind the snow-capped peaks that the state was so famous for. The fading light touched the snow casting a bluish tint on the tops of the otherwise black hills. Just as he sat down at his desk, his office phone rang.

"Echo here."

"Chief Echo, this is Travis Parker, Saralyn's daddy. I left a message earlier today and I need to know when you intend to arrest Marshall Olen. Word around town is that he's the one who killed my baby. I'm a Christian man, but if you can't do your job then don't be surprised when it gets done for you."

Tate sucked in a deep breath. "Mr. Parker, I am so sorry for your loss, and I can assure you that the department is doing everything possible to catch the person who killed Saralyn, but you need to stay out of our investigation and let us do our job. Marshall has a solid alibi for the night that Saralyn was murdered and he is not, I repeat *not*, her killer."

Silence.

"You there, Mr. Parker?"

Coughing.

"Yes, I'm here. So what you're telling me is that you won't arrest him just because he had some drinking buddy vouch for him?"

Letting out a frustrated breath, Tate explained. "Mr. Parker, Marshall Olen was in Rushville lockup the day before the crime, the night that Saralyn was murdered, and for two days after that. He was in the County Jail and that's a pretty solid alibi. I know that the townsfolk are speculating about this case, and I understand that a tragedy like this will either bring out the best or the worst in folks, but everyone has got to let the department do our job. It would be a sad situation if we arrest the killer and fail to get a conviction on a technicality, or worse yet, arrest the wrong person while the guilty party goes free. This has got to be handled by the book, and that's what I'm doing."

Sobbing.

"Mr. Parker?" No response, followed by a click disconnecting the call. Tate redialed the number to the Parker house, and then jumped in surprise when the second line on his phone rang. "Echo here."

The soft voice of a woman came on the line. "Tate, this is Sara Parker. Mr. Parker had to hang up, he's just too upset to talk. I think you should go out and check on Mr. Olen. I overheard my husband earlier on the phone and I'm afraid. I heard what you told my husband about Marshall, and, well, if he's innocent, then I'm worried that some of the locals may be out to do him harm. You understand, right Tate?"

Already pulling his Glock from a locked desk drawer and slamming it into his holster, Tate barked a reply. "Yes, Mrs. Parker, I do understand. Thank you for calling me back, but I've got to go now." Tate grabbed his cap and his cell phone. He dialed the number for Martin as he went down the stairs, got his voicemail and left a brief message. Passing the dispatch desk, Tate ordered Julie to call for back up at Marshall's house. He took the courthouse steps two at a time, jogging to his vehicle.

"This is going to be a long night," he muttered.

Turning onto the dirt road leading up to Marshall's place, Tate saw the red and blue flashing lights of two patrol cars. Standing on the front porch of Olen's small frame house, Martin was talking to a group of three men who stood in front of the house. Deputy Cook stood next to his county patrol car, at the ready if violence erupted. Nodding to the deputy as he got out of his SUV, Tate's long strides ate up the distance across the yard. Stepping up next to Martin, Tate wasn't surprised when one of the men mouthed off.

"Shouldn't you be back sittin' in your office, Echo? You don't have any authority out here. We was only going to do what one of you should have already done."

"And what would that be Mr. Long?" Tate stepped down onto the first step. "Arrest a man that wasn't anywhere near the crime scene? Or maybe you had some other brand of justice in mind."

Gerald Long, a rail thin man with a thick head of red hair took a menacing step forward.

Martin did the same. "You boys could land yourselves in some real trouble here," Martin said. "I should arrest all three of you just for thinking you could come out here and do our job, but I'm going to give you a chance to go home to your families, and leave the police work up to the police. I already told you that Marsh has a solid alibi and that is all you need to know about it. The man isn't at home, and if he was, he'd probably file charges on you for trespassing. Or worse, he might take that old shotgun his daddy left him out and fill you full of buck shot."

All three men talked at once about what they should do. When headlights swept across the yard, everyone turned and watched as Marshall's old truck bounced into the yard.

Moving fast, Tate stepped off the porch and hurried to the driver's door just as Marshall Olen shoved it open. "Hold up Marsh!" Tate demanded, and stepped close enough to smell the beer on Marshall's breath.

Taking a menacing step forward, Marshall yelled around Tate at the group of men standing near his porch. "What the hell are all you people doing in my yard? Get outta my way Echo, this is my damn house and I got a right to protect what's mine."

When Marshall tried to push past him, Tate slammed the big man face down on the hood of his truck, one arm twisted behind his back. Quietly he said, "Marshall, these men were just leaving. Seems they turned in at the wrong driveway. Won't take but just a minute for me and Crawley to clear them off your property, and while we do that I want you to have a seat in your truck. You got that Marsh?"

When the big man nodded, Tate released his arm and watched him walk to the door of the truck. Glaring at the three unwelcome visitors, Marshall fumed, "I see your damned baseball bats and I know who every one of you is. Anytime you want a piece of ol' Marsh, you just come on back when the cops aren't here, and I'll be happy to oblige you."

Tate stood in the front of Marshall's truck, as Martin shuffled the three vigilantes into their vehicle with a stern warning of what would happen if they tried anything like this again. As the tail lights of Gerald Long's truck faded, Tate motioned to Marshall.

Marshall stepped out of the truck and brushed past without a word. Stopping at the steps, he turned to look at

Tate. "I *let* you have your fucking way this time Echo, but you can't always be around, and I owe them boys something." Without waiting for a response, Marshall walked into the house, letting the door slam behind him.

Thirty minutes later, Tate pulled into the Ridge Diner closely followed by Martin in his patrol car. Stepping through the glass doors they took a booth near the door and ordered coffee.

Martin laughed, "I thought them boys were going to shit themselves when Marshall stepped out of his truck and made a beeline for them. Good thing you was there to talk him out of beating the shit out of them all, there's no way I could have held him back on my own."

Tate grinned over his coffee cup as he blew on the hot liquid. "Yeah, well, maybe we should have looked the other way and let him do just that. After all, that's what they had planned for him. You confiscate their baseball bats?"

Martin took a sip from his own cup. "Got 'em in the back of my patrol car right now. Told them boys that they'd better hope nothing bad happened to Marsh in the near future or I'd be out to pay them a visit. You get anywhere with the investigation today?"

"Nothing significant. I did spend several hours this morning searching the Department of Criminal Investigation records to see if there were any reported cases with similarities to the Parker case. Nothing logged that compares. I need that damned DNA report."

"Well the DCI does maintain the largest database of records in South Dakota," Martin said, "but we both know that not all the small town forces report things like they should."

Tate sighed, "I knew it was a long shot, but I had to look. Also checked the unrestricted FBI case files with no luck. Made another trip by Parker's house just to check the perimeter, we had a report of kids sneaking in to look at the scene. While I was there, I picked up her laptop. Found it under a stack of papers that she appeared to have been grading. System is password protected and I turned it over to the county lab to have them extract emails, and a list of websites that accessed recently, or anything else that might prove helpful."

Leaning back in the booth, Tate said, "Thanks to the hair follicle test, we know that she wasn't a regular smoker, and we know when the weed got in her system. I still believe that the Ketamine was a gift from the killer. Daniel Westhaven called and confirmed no reported cases at County Hospital involving Ketamine which pushes me to believe that I'm right about the killer using it to subdue her."

Rising to leave, Martin tossed a five dollar bill on the table and slid his hat on. "Tonight proves that the locals are like a splinter festering under the skin, just waiting to bust. They're running scared on this and tonight won't be the only call that we have to take where some dumb ass tried to take justice into his own hands. I really think you should talk to the press, get them on your side, and make a statement to the public. Give it some thought, okay?"

Tate watched Martin climb into his patrol car. *You know he's right, Echo. You've got to let the town know that you're on their side before this gets out of hand.*

Reaching for his cap, Tate slipped another five under his cup and left the diner.

CHAPTER 9

Reaching the trailhead, Gavin picked up his pace and quickly covered the short distance back to his cabin. Rushing inside, he dropped his backpack then flung his cap onto the bed. He flipped his laptop one, and slid his finger across the ID reader. Clicking the remote camera icon, he had a clear view of the happy family searching for the hidden geocache.

Gavin turned up the volume, then swore, "Damn, I should have found a close place for the camera so that I could hear them better."

Laughing, the dark-haired woman stared up at her husband. "That guy scared about ten years off my life. I wasn't expecting anyone to be out here. Guess I should have known that we weren't the only ones at the lake who'd do some caching this weekend."

"Yeah, well, I think we scared him too," the man replied. 'He was in a big hurry to get back to the campground." Glancing at the boys, he shrugged, "Probably had someone waiting for him." Both boys studied the GPS that their dad held, and stepped toward the cache site.

Turning several rocks over, they chimed in unison, "Found it!"

Gavin watched the man pull the plastic container free from its hiding spot then pull the top off. The wife reached over him, grabbing the log book out of the container. Dropping to his knees, the man sat the cache down on the ground so that the boys could see the contents.

With his eyes glued to his monitor, Gavin watched the smaller of the two boys pull the coin out and hold it up for his father to see.

"Look, Dad! Can I take it?"

Reaching out for the coin, the man turned it over in his hand. "Well, it doesn't appear to be a travel bug. Very unusual coin though. Sure, I guess you can take it, just be sure to leave something of yours in return."

Grinning, the little boy pulled an orange and yellow fishing bobber out of his pocket and dropped it into the plastic container. The man watched as his younger son dodged his brother, who had reached out to snatch the coveted prize from him.

"No fighting boys," the woman admonished with a grin. "You can both take one thing as long as you leave something in return." She turned to her husband, who was putting the cache back in its hiding spot. "We'd better get a move on if we're going to take the boat out before dinner." Holding hands, the couple moved away from the clearing, the boys followed.

Gavin watched the family leave the clearing and step out of the camera's range. He smiled and whispered, "Let the chase begin." A couple of seconds passed before a second window popped up on Gavin's computer screen. This one showed a small area map with a lighted cursor bobbing along the trail toward the campground. "That tracking coin is the smartest thing you've come up with yet Gav, and this gig with the State and National Parks system has been the best hunting ground you've ever had."

A three year contract with the State of South Dakota to install and monitor Wi-Fi in all its State and National parks gave him the access he needed to the cachers he wanted. The game had become so much more interesting.

Gavin grabbed a bottled beer from the mini-fridge, and stopped at the mirror. "Gavin, you are one smart son of a bitch. That little family has no clue that they are carrying the one thing that will lead me right to their front door." Sitting back on the worn plaid sofa in the room, he propped his feet on the coffee table, took a long draw from his beer and continued to watch his monitor.

CHAPTER 10

At Tate's request, the KCKY News van was back in the parking lot of the courthouse. Standing at the top of the steps, he watched as the rooftop antenna attached to the van rose skyward and the shaggy-haired cameraman hoisted his camera onto a tripod, and bent to adjust the focus. He walked toward the crew and took a deep breath, knowing that the camera followed him as he made his descent. Tate stopped at the bottom step and waited for the talking head from the television station to reach him.

Wes Lively smiled a plastic smile and motioned for the cameraman to zoom in for a close-up. "This is Wes Lively with KCKY News, live at the Shannon County Courthouse where we're talking to Chief of Police Tate Echo. Chief Echo, we at KCKY want to thank you for meeting with us today. We understand that you have some information to share regarding the recent homicide of Saralyn Parker."

Facing the cameras, Tate tried not to scowl. "The investigation is open and specific details continue to be confidential at this time. The Shannon County Sheriff's office is working closely with the city offices and by utilizing the manpower provided by Shannon County, we have doubled our taskforce on this investigation. I want to assure the residents of Pine Ridge that we are committed to solving this murder and that when an arrest is imminent, we will let the community know."

The newsman broke into Tate's prepared statement. "Chief Echo, do you have any suspects at this time? When do you expect an arrest?"

Tate scowled at the man. "As I stated when we spoke last week, this is an open investigation and there are sensitive details that would compromise the case should they be released too early into the investigation. My statement to the community is that while this appears to be an isolated incident, we should all remain vigilant. Keep your doors locks, and your eyes open for any suspicious activity or people, and report those to the police or sheriff's department. Do not make any attempt to approach any person or persons involved in what you might consider suspicious activity. Do not attempt to take matters into your own hands in any way. This killer is unstable and dangerous." Tate reached to shake hands with Wes, signaling that the interview was over. Surprisingly, Wes took the hint.

Tate made his way up the steps, into the courthouse and his office. The voicemail light on his phone already blinked a steady red.

CHAPTER 11

Settling in on the small front porch of his cabin, Gavin sipped a beer and leaned against the faded wooden railing. The sun drifted low over the lake; he admired its red and orange rays kissing the smooth surface and fading into the water below. The smell of charcoal fires filled the air, mixing with the aroma of pine and cedar. Somewhere in the distance he heard kids laughing as they played. As night fell on the campground, voices muted and faded as campers moved inside, settling in for the night.

"Almost time," he whispered and went inside to check his computer monitor for any changes. The green cursor blinking on his screen was stationary at a location just down the hill from his cabin. "So close." Smiling, he closed the computer. "Ready or not, here I come."

His cap on and backpack slung over one shoulder, Gavin stepped into the blackness of the night. Darkness and shadows wrapped around him, offering an eerie welcome. He slowed his steps so that anyone watching would assume that he was just another camper out for an evening stroll to the docks. Gavin slowly moved down the hill to the cabins at the lake's edge.

As the cabins came into view, he slid closer to the tree line and the protection of the sweeping branches that hung low to the ground. Settling into the woods behind cabin number three, Gavin planned to do some reconnaissance on the happy little family that he'd met earlier in the day. A few minutes later, the man and woman from the cache site stepped out onto the porch. Still holding hands, they walked a short distance to the faded wooden pier that ran out over the lake. In the daylight, the pier served as a dry place to fish and at night, Gavin supposed, it was a romantic place to take a walk.

"They are too freaking cute," he mumbled. "Too bad the little mama didn't take my coin." Gavin watched as the couple moved farther away from their cabin, and then stepped from the shadows, adjusted his backpack and casually walked to the door of the cabin.

Just a fellow camper out for a neighborly visit. He'd long ago learned that people tend to overlook the obvious. As long as you looked like you belonged, then people would assume that you did. Listening at the door he smiled at the silence that greeted him. Gavin slowly turned the door knob and entered the family's cabin, quietly closing the door behind him. "Aw, look at that."

The boys were asleep in bunk beds tucked into a corner at the back of the cabin. The older boy was on the top bunk, his back turned on the room. On the bottom bunk the smaller of the two slept soundly on one side, his legs curled tightly against his body, and one arm hanging half off the bed. A sliver of light peeking from a barely open bathroom door bathed the small room with its soft muted light.

"Little guy must be afraid of the dark," he whispered, recalling that his mother had always left the bathroom light on for him at that age. Sliding closer, Gavin smiled when he saw his coin resting in the little boy's open hand. He greedily plucked the token out of the child's hand, squeezing it tightly for a minute before he traced the etched design with one finger. A breath that he hadn't known he was holding pushed its way out of his lungs. "It's still warm with his heat. I love it."

Bending over the sleeping child, he lifted the small boy gently and placed him on one shoulder. The boy settled in and snuggled close as if he had been carried just this way a million time. The child sighed, one small arm tightening around Gavin's neck. Gavin rubbed his free hand across the child's back, soothing both the hunter and the prey.

Gavin left the cabin and slid into the darkness, taking the same trail through the underbrush that he'd walked just that morning.

Less than an hour later and freshly showered, Gavin sat in a weathered Adirondack chair, one foot propped up on the porch railing of his cabin. He watched the park entrance and wasn't surprised when two Shannon County Sheriff's cars sped through the gate.

"Down the hill they go to cabin three and two very distraught parents, probably still holding hands." Laughing at his own little joke, Gavin twisted the top off a bottle of water and took a swig before leaning back in his chair. He ran a hand over his still wet hair as he waited for the show to continue.

Minutes later, Gavin leaned forward as the headlights of another vehicle swept past the park gate. This one, a pickup, sported the South Dakota Parks Service logo and was closely followed by a small SUV with a door emblem proclaiming it to be the Shannon County K-9 unit.

The park became a beehive of activity with campers stumbling from their cabins to see what was going on. Gavin didn't move from his porch as spotlights swept back and forth through the trees, casting shadows on the ground. He smiled, enjoying the show as police officials and concerned campers made what he knew were futile efforts to look for the missing child.

Leading the group, a short and stocky female agent held what appeared to be a piece of clothing in one hand and the leash of a very large dog in the other. Catching the scent of something important, the dog made a loud sound somewhere between a bark and a howl. The massive beast took off, causing a commotion as he pulled the woman handler along. Several members of the search party followed at a brisk pace. Letting out another bark-howl, the dog took the same path around the lake that Gavin had taken twice today.

"It won't be long now." Gavin stood to go inside. "Better get inside Gav, because you're going to want a good seat once the show begins." As he'd predicted, it wasn't long at all. He stared at his laptop screen and heard the barking dog, and the people calling the kid's name through his computer speakers. He encouraged them as if it were a sporting event, "Just a little further. You're almost there." He got the primo seat to watch it all in living, or dying, as the case was, color. Gavin knew the exact instant that the boy had been found.

Eyes glued to the screen, Gavin watched the old sheriff lead the boy's father over to ID the body. He saw the man nod his head and turn away. He watched the man stumble his way back to his wife who stood at the edge of the clearing. When he reached her, the man leaned in close and said something to her. The woman's scream filled the small cabin and sent an excited chill down Gavin's back. He watched her pull away from the man and push her way past two county officers. She fell on the ground at her son's side, her cries tearing into the still night.

Gavin gasped, mocking compassion. "How touching." Two deputies pulled the woman up and away from the boy's small body, and led her back to her husband. One deputy stood with the couple while a second deputy stepped away, pulled a roll of yellow tape from his jacket, and roped the crime scene off. Another deputy forced the search team out of the clearing and out of Gavin's limited camera view. That left only the old sheriff standing near the body, solemnly guarding the lifeless child.

In the upper right corner of the computer screen, Gavin saw the man still trying to console his wife. Reaching over to his keyboard and pushing a button, Gavin centered on, and enlarged the couple on his screen. He stared at the woman, "Not so happy now, huh? Sorry about that, but he did take my coin."

The woman bent at the waist and rocked back and forth, one hand clasped over her mouth, the other covered her stomach. The man leaned over, said something to her, and she shook her head at him. He pulled his wife upward and wrapped her in his arms, turning so that she was no longer facing the mutilated body of their young son. The man closed his eyes as tears ran freely down his face. Gavin forced the computer screen back to full view, and sat back on the worn couch, "There you have it folks. A classic Hollywood moment."

With a deputies' help, the man pulled his wife out of the clearing and toward the trail, away from the crime scene. As they made their exit, three people, two men and a woman, all wearing dark-colored windbreakers stepped into the camera's range.

Gavin studied them with interest. "Ah, the Crime Scene Unit has arrived!" He grabbed another beer without taking his eyes off the screen. "Now, they're a busy group," he mumbled as the three member team split and went to work. Moving to the perimeter of the clearing, a tall, lanky man set up spotlights in various locations, turning each one on as he went. The area brightened with each light he positioned, their focused beams illuminating the entire clearing.

Lifting his been in salute, Gavin smiled, "My stage, my play and I directed it all."

One of them knelt on the ground away from the body and pulled a digital camera from a bag. He snapped shot after shot of the scene and body. He then stood near the middle of the clearing, his camera aimed and focused at the surrounding area. Turning his body, he snapped each shot, not missing one inch of the forest.

"Panoramic," Gavin hooted. "Now that's cool! Of course, there's still nothing like a live video to make the show! Too bad you guys only get stills."

Zooming in on the sheriff, still standing a few feet behind the boy, Gavin brought the officer's face full screen. Pointing at the man on his computer, Gavin laughed. Not a snicker, but a full throaty, belly shaking laugh. "The old guy's about to cry. Now that's rich. A cop with feelings!"

Adjusting the screen back to its normal size, Gavin looked on as the CSU woman pulled on a pair of latex gloves and stepped forward, kneeling next to the boy's body. Carefully picking up his little hand, she ran a small scalpel under each nail, and dropped her findings into a plastic bag.

Gavin snorted with disgust. "Lady, you are so wasting your time. By the time that kid woke all the way up he was so far into the K-hole that he didn't care what happened to him. It hit him so hard he puked and he was so little that it was almost a waste twenty five bucks to put him there."

The woman placed her scalpel into its case and pulled out what appeared to be a mini-vacuum cleaner, and ran it over the boy's clothes in a methodical pattern. Slipping the filter off the vacuum, she slid the entire thing into a separate bag and placed it inside her duffle.

Gavin reached forward to increase the volume and chuckled, "Wonder what's next in her bag of tricks?"

Stone-faced, the old Sheriff watched the investigative team work the site. Looking up, he spotted a man pushing through the brush into the clearing. The Sheriff raised his hand, and said, "Daniel, over here."

Gavin watched the younger man walk toward the sheriff. He had a jacket that said ME on it. "Coroner didn't take long on this one," Gavin whispered.

The man stepped over to the sheriff and shook his hand. Gavin strained to hear the sheriff say, "Hell of a thing to happen to a kid, Daniel. I stopped you before you saw the body to let you know that I want to keep the details quiet for now. You'll know what I mean when you see the boy."

The younger man glanced over his shoulder to where the female CSU agent bent over the child's body, and nodded.

The sheriff continued, "I don't have a lot of details yet, but Mr. Babcock, the father, called 911 almost two hours ago and said his eight-year-old son was missing. Said that he and the missus had taken a walk down to the pier, and that both boys were sound asleep when they left the cabin. When the call came in, I expected maybe the kid fell into the lake or got lost, but it only took a minute for the dog to pick up a scent and lead us here."

Gavin grinned, "Now I had to make it easy for you to find didn't I? It's not like you guys are the sharpest tools in the shed."

Nodding again, the ME moved to the child's side, kneeling down next to the tiny body and gently examining the child for any signs of life. He shook his head and checked his watch before he quietly spoke with the woman.

The man spoke to quietly for Gavin to hear. "Damn it!" he said, trying once again to boost the volume on his computer.

The ME stepped back to allow the investigator to finish her job. There was nothing that he could do except wait. Gavin watched as the ME moved to stand at the sheriff's side, and for a while, neither man spoke. The two CSU men moved in a grid search pattern, covering the entire clearing. They moved back and forth across the area methodically, each sweeping the ground with portable lights.

"I'm guessing that you noticed that the M.O. is the same as the Parker murder," the ME said, his voice low but still audible to Gavin.

"Yeah, I noticed." The sheriff's voice was gruff and hard-edged, and he shook his head as if to clear it. "What I don't get is why? Why this little boy? A serial killer usually sticks to a certain type, and the only similarity that I can come up with on this one is that Parker was an elementary teacher, and this kid was damn sure still in elementary school."

"You already let Tate know?"

"Yeah, he's on his way to the courthouse now. This one is a county investigation, but we're working them both together. I'll be taking the Babcock's back to town for the night. The boy's mother doesn't want to stay here anymore. I've got two deputies out now talking with the other guests who had cabins on the lakeshore, and those that have rentals from the lake up to here. Need to see if anyone saw or heard anything and we need statements tonight, while it's still fresh. Let me know when you're ready to move the body, okay?"

The ME nodded, took a look at the kid and said something to the sheriff that Gavin didn't catch before he disappeared off the screen. "They're wrapping it up, Gav. Show's about over for tonight, but it *has* been a good one."

The CSU lady finally stood and zipped her duffle bag, moving away from the body to talk with the two men on her team. Gavin watched the sheriff reach into his pants pocket and pull something out. "Hmm, wonder what he's up to now?" Resting his elbows on his knees, Gavin saw the old guy bend and use a pocket knife to cut the boys hands free of the red cording that they'd been tied with. Movement on the corner of the screen caught his eye and Gavin muttered, "Here comes that ME dude again."

Together the sheriff and the man in the ME's jacket lifted the boy onto an open body bag, zipped it closed, and lifted the boy onto a waiting gurney.

"Okay, show's over." Gavin his 'save' on the video file, and with a few additional keystrokes he remotely disconnected the camera, erasing any link to his computer. "Damn, I love those little mini-cams! I'm going to watch this one again and again." Gavin closed the laptop, and moved back to the chair on the porch just in time to see the ambulance leave the park followed closely by a Shannon County police car with the parents and brother of the boy huddled in the backseat.

Gavin scanned the park and noticed people gathered in small clusters speaking quietly to each other. He stopped off the porch and moved to the nearest group He made eye contact with a small brunette, smiled and asked, "What's going on?"

CHAPTER 12

In his patrol car on Park Road One, Martin Crawley rested his hands and head on the steering wheel of his cruiser while rain drummed a slow, sad song on the metal roof of his car. Sitting up, he used the back of one hand to wipe warm salty tears from his face, and cursed, "Dammit to hell...why?" Fumbling for his cell phone, Martin dialed Tate's number.

Tate was waiting when Martin pulled his cruiser into the empty parking lot of the courthouse. Watching from his office window, he saw Martin get out of his patrol car and slip the hood of his rain jacket up over his head. Before Martin reached his office door, Tate filled two mugs from the coffee maker and placed them on his desk. From a lower drawer, he pulled out an amber-tinted bottle. Tate splashed a generous amount of the dark liquid into both cups. It was Sunday and he was off duty, and even if Martin wasn't, he figured his friend needed something more than plain, black coffee.

Martin pulled the door to Tate's office closed behind him and slipped off his yellow rain slicker, and his hat, hanging them both on hooks inside the door. Taking the chair across from Tate, he slammed a manila folder on the desk, and then took a sip from the waiting cup. "What the hell is going on here Tate? First an elementary teacher is cut to ribbons, and now an eight year old kid? I can't understand how something like this could be happening in Pine Ridge. Hell, except for the summer tourist trade, this is a dying town, and we can't be home to a sick bastard that would do something like this."

Tate flipped the folder open and reached for the small flash drive bagged inside. He pulled it free and slipped the portable device into his computer. Tate waited for the photos to load while Martin continued to talk.

"It's the same guy. There are too many similarities for it to be anyone else." Martin whispered.

Pressing the computer keys that would start the slide show, Tate dreaded the harsh reality of what he was about to see. Pulling the bottle out again, Tate splashed a good amount into Martin's cup as the slides slashed on his monitor. Martin hadn't said much on the phone, but Tate had known from his strained tone and terse replies that the situation was bad. The slides moved from one grizzly scene to the next, and Tate remained silent, allowing Martin to ramble. He knew the older man needed to talk now.

"It's can't be a copycat—we never released the details on the Parker case. This kid was marked identically to Parker. He had the rings on his right forearm just like Saralyn, and his face, God Tate, his face! Can you imagine what his mother felt when she saw him? I know that the father did the ID, but there was no keeping that woman back once she knew it was her kid. No stopping her..." Martin's voice trailed off as he pressed the cup to his lips.

Tate adjusted his computer, enlarging the slides. As the screen moved from frame to frame, Tate made mental notes of the similarities in the two cases. In all of the shots, the child's hands were bound with the same red cording. He was dressed only in his underwear and a pair of Spiderman pajama bottoms that were twisted and ripped. Tate asked,

"Was this kid sexually assaulted on top of everything else?"

Yeah, he was," Martin locked eyes with Tate. "The bastard raped an eight-year-old boy."

Tate slapped the folder closed, and grabbed his hat. "Come on, buddy. I'll drive you home. We can talk about this after you've gotten some rest."

CHAPTER 13

It was time to go. Gavin stood in front of the mirror, adjusted his tie, slipped on a dark blue jacket, and then grabbed his bag from the chair. Leaving the cabin at White Clay Lake, he drove his rental car to the airport in Chadron, Nebraska, and pulled into the rental return lot. Gavin entered the airport and boarded his flight to Little Rock without incident. "I'm coming home, Mama," he whispered.

Dropping into his designated seat in the first class cabin and buckling in, Gavin caught the eye of a petite blonde stewardess and asked her for a bottle of water. As the uniformed attendant returned with his request, Gavin's chocolate eyes roved over the woman, taking in the curve of her breast and the flare of her hips. "Too bad I can't put a cache on this plane and let you find it," he muttered under his breath.

Smiling down at him, the flight attendant asked, "Did you need something else sir?"

Gavin flashed a smile, taking note of her nametag, "No, thank you, Tanya." He settled his water bottle in the cup holder attached to the seat, then leaned back and closed his eyes even though he knew that he wouldn't sleep. Knowing that he would see his other before the day was over filled him with both anticipation and dread.

As the wheels of the airplane touched the tarmac in Little Rock, Gavin pulled his cell phone from his pocket and dialed the number for the Little Rock realtor that he'd commissioned to see his mother's house. Setting up a meeting for the following morning, he pocketed the phone, and then pulled his backpack from the overhead compartment.

Gavin moved down the center isle to the exit row where Tanya was directing the first class passengers off the plane. Catching her eye as he passed, Gavin winked and gave her his best Hollywood smile. Who knew? They just might meet again.

Stepping up to the car rental counter, Gavin flashed his corporate card and a few minutes later he drove away in a red convertible. Even though he could easily afford a car, Gavin didn't own one. No car and no house, other than a remote cabin that he'd bought a few years ago, tied him to any one place for very long, and nothing, not even the credit card he'd just used, was registered in his name. Turning left on the 440 and cranking the radio up, Gavin sang along with an old George Thorogood song. "BBB...bad...bad to the bone."

A few miles down the road, Gavin sucked in a calming breath and slowed to make the turn. He arrived at the Part Central Alzheimer Center just after six p.m... He parked the rented car, and finger combed his short, dark hair as he slid out of the leather seat. Grabbing a brown paper shopping bag from the back floorboard, Gavin slid on sunglasses and walked through the double doors leading into the center.

"I'm here Mama. I'm here."

CHAPTER 14

Tate parked the SUV in the rear of the courthouse just after six the following morning, and waited as Martin pulled in. the two men had agreed to meet before hours to review the murder cases without having to field calls from the press or locals.

Leaning against his SUV, Tate waited as Martin exited his patrol car. The metallic click of the cruiser's door lock sounded out of place in the early morning stillness. Side by side they climbed the courthouse steps. Other than a nod of acknowledgement, neither man spoke. Their wordless pact to bring a killer down didn't require it.

Unlocking the wooden door to his office, Tate walked over and flipped the coffee maker on. Both men hung their coats then took opposite chairs across the desk. Before the coffee finished brewing they'd opened both case files, their resolve palpable in the small room.

"Sheriff, we've got a serial on our hands. I don't fully understand the profile on this guy, too many differences in victimology, but I know he's going to kill again if we don't stop him. On top of that, we have a serious leak somewhere in the department."

Martin glanced up. "You mean you think someone on the force is feeing detail to the locals?"

Nodding his head, Tate continued, "I do think that. I barely walked through the door last night after dropping you off when my phone started ringing. The Mayor demanding an arrest, Parker's mother wanting to know how I could let something like this happen again, and a couple more that I only half listened to. Someone at the scene brought the news back to town last night. Since it was a county investigation, that means one of your deputies, a member of the CSU team or the ME's office.

"What about the other campers? Couldn't it have been one of them?" Martin asked.

"It could have been, but I don't think that it was. People know that it has a lot of similarities to the Parker case and those campers were nowhere near the first scene. Someone is making a serious effort to undermine our investigation, and inflame the locals. Maybe that someone is actually our killer or maybe they just want us to appear inept at our jobs. Either way, it's damned frustrating to think that one of your own is working against you." Tate continued, "Right now, frustration weighs in at just over a ton, and it's all sitting right here." He bounced his fist lightly against his chest.

Picking up his coffee cup, Martin nodded. "I know exactly what you mean. I can't recall this job ever being any harder than it is right now. I called the ME's office on my way in. Daniel and Royce Wiggins were both hard at work. Royce promised me the official report on the Babcock kid by ten this morning."

Comparing notes from the field reports, medical examiner reports, and from personal observations, Tate and Martin worked uninterrupted, with Tate making notes. "Okay Martin, starting with what we do know about both cases, it's clear that there are several key pieces of evidence that are common in both murders."

Martin grunted in acknowledgement, then stood and poured them both a cup of coffee, the last in the pot. "What I know so far is that the same perp killed them both. The tattoo cuts are the same, he cut the same eye and ear on both of them, and the red cord he used to tie them both up with is the same. I don't need to wait for any damned lab results to know that."

Tate accepted the offered cup. "That's all true buddy, but it's also surface data, and as hard as it is to move past what we've seen, we've got to look deeper."

Concern lined Martin's face, "It's a hell of a lot easier to talk about forgetting what you've seen than it is to actually forget it, Tate."

"I know," Tate said. "But we've got to find this killer and the only way to do that is to focus on the facts. I once had a superior tell me that there was no room for supposition in an investigation, and that we were to deal with pragmatic information only. At the time it didn't mean much to me because I was running on raw emotion, but in the end, he was right."

Martin moved to the window. "You're right. Logically I know that, but I'm having a real hard time coming to grips with the thought that there's a serial killer right here in our little nothing of a town. And finding that little boy was something I'll never forget." Taking his seat again, martin hesitated, "So where do we go from here?"

"We've got a lot of loose ends, and we need to tie them together. We know that in both cases the victims were raped, and we know that there was overkill. That leads me to believe that either the UnSub knew both victims, or that it was personal to him in some way. We need Royce to confirm if the rape was complete or if there was pre-ejaculate only, like in the Parker rape. We also know that Babcock was killed at the lake, and that Parker had been at the lake earlier in the day before she was attacked. That's a lot of similarities."

Closing the Babcock folder, Martin leaned back, "I talked to the family last night at the scene, but they really didn't tell me anything that would help with the case. Understandable, considering what happened. They moved in from the lake last night and stayed over at the Pine ridge B&B. What say we take a ride over there and talk to them together?" Tate closed the Parker folder. "Sounds good to me, maybe they'll remember something that they forgot to tell you last night in the chaos of the moment. On the way back we can stop at the morgue and save Royce or Daniel a trip to the courthouse."

The decision made, both men grabbed their hats and coats on the way out. Even though summer was just weeks away, the chill of spring still hovered in the mountain air. In the parking lot they agreed to take the SUB since Tate was on duty for the city while Martin had worked the night shift the evening before and was officially off-duty today.

Tate turned down his radio. "You know that we can pretty much rule out that Parker's murder was linked to her marijuana use, right? I really don't have any reason to doubt what Troy Donaldson told me about that night at the party, or his own drug use. I'm pretty sure that the Babcock boy's tox report will confirm Ketamine in the bloodstream just like Saralyn parker's did. Right now, the only common denominator, other than the way they were killed, is the lake. Did you happen to ask the Babcocks if they knew Saralyn Parker?"

Martin shook his head. "The Babcocks live just across the state line in Chadron, and had come up to the lake for a long weekend. I didn't want to bring up that we'd had a similar homicide with them until we had more details. Both of them were upset, but Mrs. Babcock was on the verge of a breakdown. I had Caroline over at the B&B call Doc Shriver over once they were checked in. He gave her something to settle her down. As bad as we need answers, it didn't seem right to keep at it with her as upset as she was."

Pulling the SUV into the Pine Ridge B&B, Tate parked the vehicle. Both men sat for a minute, staring at the building, not wanting to question the grieving parents. Picking up his hat from the back seat, Martin turned to Tate. "Sitting here won't make it any easier."

CHAPTER 15

Gavin passed two women bent over and fussing with flowers in huge ceramic pots near the entrance of the Alzheimer's Center. He pushed through a set of double doors in the state of the art center where his mother lives, then wrinkled his nose and mumbled, 'Damn that nasty old people smell. Don't they ever bathe?"

Pausing, he glanced into a sunny community room, his eyes searching for her. Gavin wasn't surprised that his mother was not one of a gaggle of blue haired old women clustered around a TV watching some reality show.

Shaking his head, he muttered in frustration, "Shit. I pay a fortune for this place, and she won't leave her room." Frozen in the doorway, Gavin closed his eyes, willing his mother to appear. *You used to love flowers Mama, you could be outside right now. Those women wouldn't care about your scars. They wouldn't Mama, they'd love you, just like I do.* Winking at an old woman who stopped watching television to look up at him with a searching blank stare, Gavin moved through the elaborately decorated lobby and into the heart of the center. Not slowing, he passed the reception desk and took a left down a long, sterile, white-painted hallway. As he approached the last door on the wing, Gavin's steps slowed.

His mother's room.

Gavin paused outside the door to Silvia Wheeler's room and took a deep breath, letting it out slowly. Pasting a smile on his face, he pushed into the room. At first he thought his mother was sleeping, but as he took a step closer to the bed, her eye fluttered open. For a brief moment, he caught the fear in her expression before she was swallowed back into the nothingness that she lived in. Standing next to the bed, Gavin stooped to kiss his mother's forehead.

Gavin grasped her small, blue-veined, and paper-thin hand, and asked, "How are you Mama? It's me Gavin, remember?"

Nothing. Not one damn word.

Trying again, Gavin asked, "Did you like the new clothes that I had sent over for you? You look really pretty today, Mama."

More nothing.

Pulling a chair close to his mother's bed, Gavin sat and reached over to push Silvia's thin, graying hair back from her forehead, careful not to disturb the black patch that she insisted on wearing over one eye to cover her scar.

"You're due a haircut, Mama. I'll get someone over here to take care of that for you. I brought you a present today, want to see?" Reaching into the shopping bag, Gavin pulled out a soft bodied baby doll with dark curly hair and eyes that opened and closed.

Silvia turned to look at her son for the first time since he'd entered the room. She reached out for the doll and snatched it from Gavin's hands, pulling it tightly to her chest.

Gavin chuckled, "You like that Mama?"

Smiling, Silvia reached out to touch Gavin's face lightly with one hand. Haltingly she spoke, "B-baby."

Covering her hand with his own, much larger one, Gavin

closed his eyes, remembering a different mother. He turned his mother's hand over in his own and pushed the sleeve of her dress up, revealing a faded tattoo. Using one finger, he traced the three rings on her arm.

"One for each of us, huh, Mama? Our family, joined forever, just like the circles on your arm." Gavin pushed the sleeve down to cover the tattoo and fought to control his anger. Leaning forward he spoke quietly into her good ear. "You should have gotten only two rings, Mama. That bastard didn't deserve one. He didn't deserve us either. You know he did this to you." Gavin ran a hand over the scar that marked her missing ear. His father had cut the ear off in one of his drunken rages. It was a wonder she survived the man.

Silvia slid her hand free from Gavin's grasp, and pulled her new baby closer. She closed her eye and gently rubbed the doll's back in a soothing motion.

Leaning back in his chair, Gavin sighed. It was getting harder to come here and pretend that she would ever be normal again. The blank look on her face was proof enough without the black patch covering her right eye. The patch hid the scars of a tortured life spent with a bastard of a man, but nothing could ever cover that look. "If the fucker wasn't already in hell, I'd give him a one way ticket there myself, Mama."

No response.

Gavin stood. "I've got to go Mama, but I'll be back. I've got work to do. Got to pay those bills, you know. I'll be back real soon. I love you, Mama."

No response.

Gavin made a quick stop at a local liquor store and then checked into a hotel two blocks away from the center. Draining his third glass of whisky, he opened his computer for a little late night freak show before bed.

CHAPTER 16

Entering the B&B, both Tate and Martin respectfully removed their hats and stood at a small table that Caroline Spencer used as her registration desk. Before Tate could ring the silver-plated 1950's era school bell sitting on the polished wood table, a large woman with graying hair pushed through a pail of swinging doors that lead into the kitchen. Wiping her floured hands on an apron covered with teacups and roses, Caroline Spencer stepped forward to greet the two lawmen.

"I suppose you're here to see the Babcocks. Just a shame, I tell you, a shame what those poor folks are going through."

Even though the visit was a somber one, Tate had to fight back a smile. Getting a word in with Caroline in the room was almost impossible, and today was not going to be different.

"Well, you boys go on into the sitting room and take a chair. I'll let the mister know that you're here. Now that poor woman, if she's finally asleep, you will not wake her up. You hear me, boys?"

Realizing that she had paused to take a much needed breath, Tate jumped in. "Caroline, we'll do our best not to upset Mrs. Babcock, but we do need to speak with them both."

Giving the men a hard look and a brisk nod, Caroline turned and began a slow climb up creaking stairs to the second floor landing. Still talking, her voice carried down to Tate and Martin. "Just a shame I tell you. A sad, sad shame."

Martin took a seat in a faded blue wingback chair while Tate looked out a lace covered window into the back yard Moments later, the stairs creaked in protest, announcing Caroline's return. She had the remaining Babcock child pulled close to her side. Shooting a frown Tate's way and speaking quietly to the boy, she steered him through the bat-wing doors into the kitchen, giving Tate and Martin some much needed privacy to speak with his parents. The kitchen doors were still moving when both Mr. and Mrs. Babcock came down the stairs. Mr. Babcock's arm curved protectively around his wife's waist, holding her up as they entered the small sitting room. They sat side-by-side on the sofa.

Martin shook hands with the parents. He spoke in a hushed tone to the couple, "Mr. and Mrs. Babcock, this is Tate Echo, he's the police chief of Pine Ridge, and we're working the case jointly."

Tate stepped forward and shook hands with the grieving couple, expressing his sympathy for the loss of their child. He took a seat across from the Babcock's and pulled his notepad out, waiting for Martin to open the dialogue.

Measuring his words carefully so as not to further upset the grieving couple, Martin said, "Tell us about your day yesterday, beginning from the time you arrived at the lake until you noticed that your son was missing."

Mr. Babcock cleared his throat. "We got to the lake about nine yesterday morning and checked in. Went to the cabin and unloaded our stuff, and then me and the boys took a boat out on the lake." Choking back a sob, he continued, "We only caught a couple fish, but Justin caught the biggest one and he...he couldn't wait to tell his mom." Reaching out in silent support, Mrs. Babcock caught her husband's hand, holding it tightly in both of hers.

Seeing the couple struggle to maintain their composure, Tate waited before speaking, giving them a minute to collect themselves and their thoughts "After you came I from the lake, what did you do then?"

Mrs. Babcock pulled a wadded up tissue from her hand and blew her nose. She lifted a tear-stained face to meet Tate's gaze. "Lun...lunch. We took sandwiches down to the dock so that I could see the fish. The boys had left them tied to the dock." Large tears pooled in her eyes and spilled down her cheeks. Stumbling over her words she tried to continue, "My baby's last lun..."

Mr. Babcock wrapped his arms around his wife and pulled her close as she sobbed. Shaking her head, she pushed away from her husband and turned to face Tat and Martin. In a burst of strength, she firmly said, "I want you to find whoever did this. I need to..."

Martin spoke up, "We intend to find Justin's killer, ma'am. I promise that we—"

Tate cut Martin off before he could make promises that they might not be able to keep. "Mr. and Mrs. Babcock, we'll do everything in our power to make sure that we catch the killer." Steering the conversation back to a more productive line of questioning, Tate added, "Now what did you do after lunch?"

Mr. Babcock continued, "We hiked around the lake and did some geocaching."

Tate looked up at this. "Geocaching? That's when you use a GPS to play a high tech game of hide and seek, right?"

Mr. Babcock opened his mouth to speak but stopped when his wife excitedly grabbed the sleeve of his shirt and shook his arm.

"Richard! Oh my God, Richard, oh God."

"What is it? What's wrong?" He took his wife by the arm.

Jumping up from her seat on the couch, Mrs. Babcock took a few steps away from the sofa, wrapping her arms around her middle she turned and faced the three men in the room. "Richard, the place where Justin was. The place that they found Justin, that's where we found the cache yesterday afternoon. And *that* man. You know, that man who was in such a hurry. Oh Richard, what if he took Justin?" Collapsing back on the couch and burying her hands in her face, Mrs. Babcock's shoulders shook; her sobs barely audible through her hands.

Giving her a minute, Martin finally spoke up, "Tell us more about the geocaching, and this man you mentioned."

Mr. Babcock explained that they'd used their laptop to search the geocaching website for caches in the lake area before programming them into their GPS, and going out to search for them.

Tate took notes and wrote down the web address for the geocaching site, as well as the Babcock's log in ID and password so that he could log into their account. "Now I need you to think back to the man you met there and describe him for me. What color hair did he have? How was he dressed? Anything that you can think of could be helpful."

Questions and answers went back and forth, and Tate and Martin didn't notice the passing of time until the third time that Caroline stuck her head in to announce lunch. Deciding it was time to give the family a break, both men stood to leave.

Tate shook hands with Mr. Babcock, and handed him a business card. "Give me a call if you remember anything else, and we'll touch base with you again before you leave Pine Ridge."

Mr. Babcock nodded. "We want to go home, but we're waiting." His voice broke, "We're waiting for Justin."

Back in the SUV, Tate turned to Martin. "The interview took longer than I thought it would, but I think we have some good information. I'm betting that the ME has already sent the Babcock report over to your office. What say we grab a burger from the diner, and head back to the courthouse?"

Martin nodded "Sounds like a plan to me."

Ten minutes later, the bell over the diner door clanged a greeting as Martin and Tate entered. Stepping up to the counter near an old fashioned cash register, Tate made eye contact through a rectangular opening behind the counter with a huge, thick necked man in the kitchen. Burt Walker had been a cook in the Navy before retiring and moving to Pine Ridge over twenty years ago. Tate nodded a greeting and Burt nodded back.

Burt yelled, "Customers out front, girl!"

Reva hurried through the swinging door that connected the kitchen to the dining area, she wiped her hands on a faded dish towel as she went. She slung the towel over one shoulder and smiled, "Hello, Tate. Martin." Pulling a pad from her apron pocket, she asked, "What'll you boys have today?"

Martin smiled back at her, "Just a couple burgers and some rings, to go."

"Reva made a note on her pad and ripped the top sheet off, then she clipped the order to a stainless wheel spinning it toward the kitchen for Burt. "Get you something to drink while you wait?"

Tate shook his head, "No, thanks. I do have a questions for you though. You ever hear of geocaching?'

Reva nodded, "Sure. It's a lot of fun. Why do you ask?"

Ignoring her question, Tate took a seat on a round swivel stool at the bar. "You and Saralyn ever do any caching out at the lake?"

"Yeah, we did. Me and Saralyn both like looking for caches. Her daddy gave her a GPS for Christmas last year, and we spent just about all our free time looking for them around Pine Ridge. You wouldn't believe how man—"

Tate interrupted her, "Any chance that you were looking for caches the day that Saralyn was murdered?"

Looking thoughtful, Reva paused a minute, then replied, "Well, yeah. We did go caching out at the lake that day."

"Order up!" Burt yelled from the kitchen.

Reva pulled a brown paper bag from the window and moved to the decades old cash register to ring up the order. Holding one finger up, she said, "Let me get this order out for Mr. Brownlee, and I'll be right back with you." She stepped around the counter with the bag in and hand, and walked toward an elderly man who sat near the door. Smiling down at him, Reva waited while he moved a three-legged cane aside and pulled some cash from his pocket.

Finished with her customer, Reva returned to the two lawmen at the counter. "He is just the sweetest little thing. Comes in once a week and takes burgers home for him and Mrs. Brownlee. You know, she can't get out much anymore. Burt always gives them extra..." Stopping mid-sentence, she seemed to remember that Tate and Martin were there on business. "Oh my, I'm sorry, what was it you wanted to ask me about?"

After giving her the description of the man the Babcock's met while they were caching, Tate asked, "Reva, are you sure you didn't see anyone matching this man's description while you were caching that day?"

"No, like I already told you, we didn't talk to anyone that day, other than when we signed in at the gate. You thinking that geocaching had something to do with Saralyn's murder?"

Martin cut in, "We're not sure, but it's something that we're looking into."

Reva's eyes clouded, "I heard about that kid that died out at the lake. Was he caching too?"

Catching the young woman's eye, Tate asked, "What exactly did you hear about Justin Babcock's death?"

Reva looked around to make sure that no one else in the diner could hear. "Several of the regulars were talking about it this morning over coffee. Said he was cut up just like Saralyn."

"And what else did they say? Anything?" Tate queried.

Her voice dropped lower. "Well, Tate, they said that you weren't doing a damn thing to catch the killer." She turned her eyes away. "And then Tim Webber said that some of them were going to talk to Mayor Hooper about having you replaced as chief, but Walt Mabry said they should leave things alone and let you do your job."

"Order up!" Burt yelled from behind them. Another brown paper bag appeared in the opening between the kitchen and dining area, and Reva pulled it down, glancing at the order for stapled to it, she said, "This one's yours."

Tate took the paper bag full of burgers and slid some bills over to Reva. "I appreciate you telling me that, Reva. You know that we can't talk about the Babcock case any more than we can go into the details of Saralyn's murder, but we are working on both cases, and we will do our best to catch this guy. You have to believe that."

"I believe you; it's just that some of the folks around town think that because you come back to Pine Ridge that you must not have been a very good FBI guy. I mean, who would quit the FBI to work here?'

Tate gritted his teeth to keep from cursing. "I don't have time to go into my life with you, or anyone else right now. I left the FBI for personal reasons that nothing to do with my work performance. This is where I grew up, it's where my family is, and that's why I came back to Pine Ridge. I gotta go, but first, I need you to promise me that you won't forget our conversation about things that you might overhear at work or in town, okay?"

Her eyes grew wide. She dropped her voice even lower and said, "Yeah, Tate, I do remember...I do."

A few minutes later, Tate and Martin sat in Tate's office eating their burgers and comparing the ME reports from the Parker and Babcock cases.

"No surprise here," Tate said between bites. "We already knew that it was the same guy, the signature is too strong to think otherwise. I expected that we would see Ketamine on the tox report, and with no trace of marijuana on the report, it further confirms our conclusions regarding Parker's drug use. I don't fully understand the incomplete rape. Daniel suggested that something forced him to stop before he could finish, but since he called in the murder at Parker's that can't be right either. Bastard must not be able to get off."

Martin shook his head. "I don't get it. Why did he have to drug the kit? I know he would have had to give Saralyn something to subdue her, but this was just a little boy. For that matter, why the change in victimology? Why a kid at all?"

Standing to refill his coffee cup, Tate raised the half-full pot, silently asking Martin if he wanted more as well. He did. Tate thought aloud for a moment, "It's true that most killers will stick to the same type of victim, but it's not a hard rule. I reached the crime databases looking for killers that fit the M.O. using female victims, but now I need to go back and broaden the search. In fact, I think it's time to call the big guns and ask for some under the radar help."

Martin raised a brow, "You still got connections at the FBI?"

Tate nodded. "I don't want to make an official request for help from the bureau just yet. I don't want them sending a team to take over the investigation since that might scare our killer off. But I do know a very good criminal profiler who won't ask too many questions if I call her for help."

CHAPTER 17

Gavin stood in the shower of his hotel room and tried not to think about the scheduled meeting with the realtor later that morning. He cursed. "Why the hell did I agree to meet at the house? I hate that fucking house."

He grabbed a towel and quickly dried himself, then stared at his reflection in the mirror. Water dripped from his short hair onto his shoulders, and ran in in little rivers down his chest to be sucked into the towel now wrapped at his waist. Leaning forward, he met his own stare in the mirror and wanted, "Get a grip Gav. It's no big deal, just an old house that you need to unload. Right. It's just a viper pit of memories you don't need, and the quicker you unload it, the quicker you can forget it."

Thirty minutes later, Gavin turned the red convertible into the driveway of his childhood home. He stepped out and looked at the place. A post WWII cottage, a little worse for wear, but it was mostly how he remembered it. He stared at the faded white exterior and the gray painted porch. *Yard looks good. Guess that kid next door takes his job pretty seriously.*

Pushing back dark memories of this house and his childhood, Gavin took the steps of the porch two at a time. He slid a new key into the lock of the freshly painted front door and let it swing inward. He stepped over the threshold just as he'd done a million times before in his life.

The house smelled of bleach and lemons. *Guess the cleaning service did their thing, too.* Gavin stopped in the blue painted living room and stared at the old, worn furniture there. A green vinyl covered sofa flanked by two tables that were straight from the 70's, a scarred coffee table in front of the sofa was where he'd did homework as a child. In the corner sat his father's recliner.

A blast from the past, Gav. Only it wasn't so much fun. Stepping to what was once his father's favorite chair, Gavin flopped down and pushed back to extend the foot rest.

Gavin laughed, the sound echoed in the small house, "What do you think of that old man?" Gavin demanded aloud. "I'm sitting in your chair today while you rot in hell." He pushed out of the aged recliner without putting the foot rest down, and laughed again, "That used to drive you crazy, didn't it old man?"

Gavin turned to inspect the kitchen. His mother had painted the kitchen yellow when he was twelve. The paint had lightened with age and was chipped around the doorway, but overall it still looked the same. The cabinets had been emptied and the counters cleaned. There was a note on the bar addressed to Mr. Wheeler and Gavin opened it. The maid service he'd hired to clean the house had boxed the kitchen and other personal items left behind, and placed them in the basement for his review.

Gavin jammed the note into his jacket pocket as he walked to the kitchen stairs that led down to the basement. *That's right, old man. I'm Mr. Wheeler now. You never even existed.* Halfway down the dusty wooden stairs, Gavin stopped. *Damn I hate this basement. Used to flood every spring and while I was down here shoveling dirty water, that stupid bastard just sat on the steps and watched.* He could still hear his daddy's voice, "time to empty the bucket boy. You missed a spot boy. Hurry your lazy ass up boy!"

He shook his head and struggled to push away a different set of memories. Darker, more sinister memories. He sank down on the next to the last step.

Gavin saw his daddy standing in the shed out back, heard his voice, smelled his sweat.

"Time to pay the bills boy. You got any money?"

He'd been seven years old the first time he'd heard that question.

"You gotta pay for your keep boy, come on over here and let me see if you have any money in those pockets."

Gavin couldn't stop the memories now; they took control and consumed him. Rocking on the steps, he felt his old man sliding a big dirty hand into the pocket of his shorts.

"No change in there, but wait, what's that I feel? Maybe a little folding money all rolled up?"

"Stop laughing, you ugly bastard!" Gavin heard his own voice tear through the fog of the past, but it wasn't strong enough. He wasn't strong enough.

"Pull those shorts down and show me that roll of money boy. I've got a big roll of money myself. Come over here and I'll show it to you. That's it, just relax. It won't take long to pay those bills."

"I've got money. That hurts! Stop! Oh, please stop!" Gavin heard his voice begging, saw his own tear-stained face, felt the pain. Rocking harder, he begged the memories to leave him, let him be.

"I'll stop in a minute, before it gets messy. You know

what messy is don't you boy?"

"Mr. Wheeler! You in here, Mr. Wheeler?" the high-pitched voice of a woman pulled Gavin back to the present.

"Bastard," Gavin hissed. He sat for a moment composing himself, and then slowly he climbed the stairs.

"Ah, there you are, Mr. Wheeler!" The middle-aged realtor said. "I see that you've had the house all cleaned up and those planters of ivy on the porch really were just the best touch."

With a smile that didn't reach any further than his lips, Gavin approached the irritating woman and shook hands.

She pulled her bag up on her shoulder and chattered, "Now, I think that with just a few more improvements, we should be able to get a fair price for the house."

Gavin frowned, "No."

"Now, whatever do you mean, Mr. Wheeler? New interior paint and flooring would go a long way in getting you a higher bid. Don't you want to get a good price for the house? I think..."

"Sell the house as is," Gavin interrupted. "I've only kept it this long because it belonged to my mother. I don't ever intend to step foot in it again."

A frown creased the woman's forehead and he recognized that she was thinking of her commission. "Twelve percent," Gavin barked. "Sell the house in sixty days, and your commission more than doubles what it would normally be. That should more than make up for any loss on the asking price."

Her beady eyes widened at his proclamation, then narrowed appreciatively, a slow smile turning her lips upward. Gavin swore he could see the calculator in her brain clicking away at the numbers.

Pulling some papers from a briefcase sitting on the floor, Gavin saw her smile widen as she bent away from him. Keeping her tone flat, the woman drawled, "Well, okay Mr. Wheeler, as long as you know that we probably won't be getting everything that we could for the property."

Motioning her to follow, Gavin took a seat at the kitchen table and pulled a pen from his inner jacket pocket. "Where do I sign?"

Gavin pulled the door closed behind him and stepped out of the house for the last time. He sucked in the cool spring air, feeling the pressure in his chest lift a little. With the turn of a key he locked away the unwanted memories of his past. He pressed the house key and his business card into the realtor's paper-white hand, and instructed her to e-mail him any necessary paperwork as he didn't plan to return to Little Rock for several months. He stood on the porch and watched as she got in her car, giving him a jaunty little wave before backing out of the drive.

"Silly bitch."

Gavin watched the realtor's car turn the corner and made sure it was out of sight before he moved down the narrow cement steps of the porch and walked around the side of the house to the back yard. He paused under a giant oak tree, and looked around. It was so familiar, so very familiar. Nothing had changed. *How many hours had he spent out here when his daddy was passed out drunk in front of the television?*

Moving through the yard, he slid into a copse of pine trees lining the back of the property. Without any thought at all, he took an old trail leading through the woods to a small stream where he'd played as a boy. Gavin stood on the rocky edge of the stream. His eyes moved across to the opposite bank and then landed on a pine covered hillside. "They're all still here," he whispered.

A slow smile spread across his face. He needed their comfort all those years ago, and knowing they were still here, were still his, gave him comfort once again. It started with a bird that broke its wing and was soon joined by another, and then another. Then a squirrel or two and many cats of all colors, some from the neighborhood and some were strays. Then, there was the old man's dog. That one gave him such a rush, such power. Knowing he'd hurt the old man just a little bit was something for a small boy. Even now, Gavin felt his penis harden at the thought of that dog's blood flowing into the creek. The fear, adrenalin and pure excitement of that moment gave him a high like no other. No one could take them from him; each and every kill scabbed over old wounds, keeping them hidden, at least for a while. He could feel the need building once again. It would be long until he needed that high again.

He retraced his steps through the woods and yard without giving the house another look, and slid into the convertible. He turned the radio up to drown out his thoughts, and reached for the button to lower the convertible top. As the top of the car slid down and the warm sunshine touched his face, Gavin relaxed, letting the music and wind pull him back to the present.

Back at the hotel, he turned the car onto the paved, red-brick driveway and slid to a smooth stop near the entrance. The colonnade was shaded and cool. The front of the eight story building was tastefully decorated with large planters and iron benches that screamed 'stay here!' to passing travelers. Not slowing to lock the car or speak with the doorman, Gavin entered the hotel and took the stairs two at a time until he reached the second floor. *Time to move on, Gav. You've seen enough of the old home town to last a lifetime.*

He quickly packed, slid his computer into the leather carrying case and zipped it closed. Grabbing his duffle and backpack, he returned to the lobby to check out. *One more stop and you're out of here.* He thought.

Gavin drove the short distance to the Alzheimer's unit, and briskly walked down the barren hallway to his mother's room. He pushed the door open and was surprised to see her sitting on a small stool in front of a mirrored dressing table.

"Mama?" Gavin moved to stand behind her. She looked up at his reflection.

"Baby. My Baby," she stammered.

At first, Gavin thought she meant him, but then saw the doll in her arms. Squatting so that he was eye level with her, Gavin grinned, "That's right, Mama." Pointing to the doll, he said, "That's your baby." He smiled up at her and said, "I've got work to do, mama, but I'll be back soon to see you and the baby." Gavin kissed his mother on the forehead, ignoring that she flinched at the touch of his lips.

CHAPTER 18

Tate pulled into the driveway just after seven in the evening, grabbing his mail on the way in. He sorted through the envelopes as he walked. *Junk mail. Well, I guess that's better than bills.* Pushing the play button on his answering machine, he listened as some man tried to sell him insurance, and then hit delete. The next message boomed the mayor's voice into the room; he left his name and number, but no message.

Delete.

Tate dropped the junk mail into a small, round plastic trash can then walked through the living room and into his small kitchen. He stood at the open refrigerator and sighed before pulling out a package of ham, and the mayo. *Should've stopped at the diner or called Mom. Guess a sandwich will have to do.* Pulling bread out of a plastic bag, Tate brought it to his nose and sniffed, before shrugging and spreading the mayo on. He slapped the sandwich together and put it on a paper plate from a stack near the sink. Tate grabbed a beer as he returned the ham to the fridge. Sliding the patio door open, he took a seat at a rough-hewed pine table on the deck. His feast, if you could call it that, in front of him.

He closed his eyes and soaked in the peaceful silence of his back yard, then wondered where the killer was tonight. Was he planning another kill, or would the phone ring tonight with another gruesome discovery?

"God, I hope not," he whispered. He finished the sandwich and grabbed another beer. Tate snatched his cell from the counter on his way back outside. *No sense putting it off any longer, Echo.* Punching in ten very familiar numbers, Tate waited while the call connected.

Emma answered on the second ring. "Tate?"

He still loved the almost breathless way that she said his name. He smiled, remembering when he could make her whisper more than just his name in that same soft and husky voice. "Yeah Em, it's me. How've you been?"

"I'm fine. Is everything okay? Everyone okay? I mean your daddy—" a pause. "Karlee?"

"Everyone is fine, Em. That's not why I'm calling."

She sighed, "If everyone is fine, then why are you calling me Tate? I haven't heard from you in four months and after the way our last call ended, I wasn't sure if I'd ever hear from you again unless someone died."

Ah, she hadn't forgotten the last call, and he wondered if he'd made the right choice to call her now. Before he could stop himself, Tate asked, "You still seeing that guy Jay or Ray, or whatever the hell his name is?" Tate heard Emma suck in a sharp breath and blow it out. He knew he's said the wrong thing, but when it came to Emma, he just couldn't seem to stop himself. He'd always thought that someday, well, that they'd manage to work it out. She was his.

"Jay, his name is Jay, and no, I'm not still seeing him. But Tate, if I want to see someone, then I can do that. We are divorced, remember?"

"Em, I'm sorry. I know we're divorced. Hell, I remember it every single day when I wake up in an empty bed. Look, I didn't call to fight with you. I have a problem that I want to run past you; a killer problem."

"So what's going on?" Emma asked.

Without holding back any details, Tate spent the next half hour relaying the scant information that he had on the two murders.

Emma listened without interrupting, and when Tate finished, she said, "Sounds like you have a serial on your hands Tate. So, are you going to make a formal request for assistance from the Bureau?"

"No, I'm not putting in a formal request just yet Pine Ridge expects e to handle this, and if I don't, well let's just say that it will further undermine their confidence in my abilities as chief of police here, and right now the town is running scared as it is."

"Hmm...I see. So what kind of help do you want from me?"

"I was actually hoping that you would do some off the radar research for me. My resources are a little more limited than yours."

Emma laughed. "I'll do a little database creeping and give you a call in a day or two."

God, he'd missed the way she laughs. Rich and throaty, her laugh is sexy as hell. Just like the rest of her.

Tate disconnected the call and was surprised when the phone immediately rang. "Echo here."

"Tate, this is Davis over at the County Lab. We got that report you wanted on Parker's computer, and I was wondering if you wanted me to fax it or e-mail it to you tonight? Pretty standard stuff from my perspective, nothing unusual or suspicious."

Tate elbowed the patio door open, and went into the kitchen to deposit his empty plate as he talked, "That would be great. E-mail the report to me, and then send a hard copy to my office please. I'd like to review the findings as soon as possible."

Tate went down the hall to his home office and booted up his computer. *Might as well call Mayor Hooper while I wait.*

Within seconds, the mayor's voice boomed on the line, "It's about damn time you returned my call Echo."

"Sorry about that, Mayor, but despite public opinion, I don't spend all my time at my desk. I do have several leads that we are actively pursuing."

"Yeah, well, I need to know what's going on. Every damn time I step out of my office, I have some concerned citizen stopping me to find out when I'm going to pull you and put a competent chief in your office, or telling me that if I don't do something about these murders that I won't get their vote. It's hard to support your department or your position when I don't know what the hell's going on."

Bringing the Mayor up to speed on the geocaching angle, Tate told him that he had a buddy with the FBI checking serial killer profiles in databases that normal police departments didn't have access to. "I don't want that information shared, so please keep it just between the two of us," he said.

Hearing that Tate still had friends with the FBI seemed to pacify the mayor, and they hung up on slightly better terms.

Tate clicked the mail icon on his computer, and opened the new file that David had just sent. Scrolling through the list of files on Saralyn's computer, Tate agreed that it was pretty standard stuff for a young woman. Moving to a roster of her e-mails for the last sixty days, he really wasn't surprised when there wasn't anything incriminating or suspicious there either. Tate quickly scanned a listing of recently accessed websites and found what he was looking for.

"Bingo," he said and printed the list out. He grabbed the pages off the printer and rummaged through a desk drawer until he found a blue highlighter. Tate scanned the list, pausing to highlight each entry for the geocaching website. It was the same one the Babcock's used. Once all the entries were noted, he called Martin's cell.

"Sheriff Crawley," Martin said.

Sliding his chair back from the desk, Tate propped his feet up on one corner, "It's me. I got the reports back on parker's computer tonight and thought you'd want to know."

"So what'd you find" Anything there going to help us catch this guy?"

"Not sure, but she did regularly access the same geocaching website as the Babcock's. Twenty-three entries in the last sixty days. Reva didn't act like they went caching that many times. Has me wondering if Saralyn went with anyone else. Of course, if you think about the fact that she went on the site once to locate the caches, and then again to log the finds, it's only about twelve trips, but that is still quite a bit.

"Yep," Martin agreed. "I'll stop by the diner in the morning on my way in and ask Reva to pull out a calendar and figure out how many times they went in the last two months."

"That'd be great. While you're there, ask her if she knows anyone else that Saralyn might have cached with, or if Saralyn ever went alone." Tate hesitated a minute, then cleared his throat. "I also talked to a friend in the Bureau and she's going to do some research on her end for us. Should hear back from her in a day or two."

That's great news. We can use all the help we can get with this case."

Tate sighed, relieved that Martin didn't pelt him with questions about Emma. He wasn't sure he was ready to answer them just yet.

CHAPTER 19

By eight thirty the following morning, Martin and Tate had shared a pot of coffee and a bag of cinnamon rolls from the diner. After logging into the Babcock's geocaching account and scanning the finds that Mr. Babcock had logged, they found three entries from the lake in the last two months.

"We need Parker's log in and password so that we can compare the sites that the Babcock's went to with those that Saralyn and Reva went to," Martin said.

"Yeah I know," Tate replied. "I already called our IT guy to see if he could somehow back into that information, and I've got a call out to the geocaching website owner asking that they provide us with that as well. Pretty sure they're going to try and put me off, based on their privacy statement. If they do, I'll get a warrant."

Martin drained the last of his coffee. "Let me know when you hear back from them. Judge Walker owes me a favor and if we need a warrant, I'll call him for it. I've been thinking about your theory that there's a leak in the department. I went back over the Parker file, and even though the murder happened in town, I did have a responder show up at the scene for back-up. Wanna guess who it was?"

"I was pretty busy that night, and I haven't had time to check the sign in from the scene, but if I were guessing, I'd have to say Chad Green."

"Well, you're almost right. It was Pete Green. Seems Chad's daddy might be the leak. He's the only officer that was at both scenes, and since his wife died last year, he's a regular at the diner."

Slamming his hand against his desk, Tate swore, "Son of a bitch. If he's feeding details to the public, I will make his life a living hell."

"Now Tate, you know you can't just walk up to a man and accuse him of something like that. He'd never admit to it. He's got over twenty years on the county force, and he's well-liked and respected around town." Martin grinned, "I do have a plan though, want to hear it?" when Tate nodded, Martin continued, "I just reassigned Pete to a new partner. Told him I need an experienced officer with one of the newer recruits. Stating today he's riding with Amy Moorehouse, but what he doesn't know is that Amy is on loan from the State Capitol Division of Internal Affairs."

Tate laughed, "You are one sneaky SOB, Martin."

"I can't have someone doing that kind of crap on the team. If he's the leak then Amy will find out. She's got plans to stick with him like syrup on a pancake. I'll keep you posted on what she reports." Martin grabbed his hat and left.

The rest of the day, Tate jumped every time the phone rang. He told himself that he hoped it would be the lab or the geocaching web owner returning his call, but he really hoped that it would be Emma. He tried to convince himself that it was information on the case that he needed, but Tate was smart enough to realize that he just wanted to hear her voice. He reached for the phone, but stopped. *Don't do it, Echo. Picking up that phone is only going to make you look like a love sick ass. Once call and you already forgot to leave the past alone like you promised yourself you would.*

Tate glanced at the clock. Six p.m. He slid into his jacket and grabbed his cap to leave when his cell phone rang.

"Tate, it's Emma. I'm at the Pine Ridge airport. How long will it take you to get here and pick me up?"

Stunned, Tate stuttered, "Em, you know I'll come and get you, hell I'd drive to Virginia to get you if that's what you wanted, but why are you here? Why are you in Pine Ridge?"

Laughing nervously, Emma said, "I'm on a three week leave from the Bureau, and I thought about how long it had been since I've seen you...seen your parents." She paused, "Just come get me, okay?"

Pulling the door closed, Tate headed to the parking lot as they talked. "I'm on my way. But if you're here because of the murders, then you can just turn around and take your pretty little ass back to Virginia."

This time, Emma laughed a full throaty laugh that had Tate smiling. He imagined her with her head tilted back, her long hair flowing down her back.

"Just come get me. I have a few weeks off, and I wanted to see you. It's been over a year, you know. I don't know if I still have a pretty little tail or not, so get out here and pick me up. We can sort out the rest later."

Emma Gage-Echo pulled her bag off the luggage carousel at the Pine Ridge Airport, and slid the handle up, dragging it behind her as she slipped out the glass double doors of the airport and stood in the passenger pick-up area. Looking at the black hills in the distance, she thought that Tate had been right to leave the FBI and come back here. "This is where he belongs," she whispered.

Tate had been a great agent, and they'd been an amazing team until they'd fallen in love. Frustrated that she would even think the word 'love,' Emma stamped her foot on the smooth pavement and whispered to herself, "Emma Gage-Echo don't you dare forget that Tate is off limits. Do *not* forget how it was in the end. That sweet man turned into an absolute idiot, remember?"

She remembered alright. Every time she'd pulled a case, he freaked out, and his constant worrying had made them both crazy until finally they'd split apart like a tree struck by lightning; two pieces belonging together, but separated by hot jagged edges that no longer fit.

Emma caught sight of Tate's SUV and watched while he steered over to the curb. All six feet plus of him unfolded from the vehicle. *Damn he looks good.* A little tremor skittered down her back. Unable to move, Emma stared as Tate slid his cap on and strode toward her.

One step His hair was a little long, the dark strands touching the collar of his brown uniform shirt.

Two steps. His grey eyes were intense and questioning as they locked with hers.

Three steps. Emma had always loved those eyes—and those long 'belonged on a woman' lashes that framed them.

Four steps. *Get a grip Emma, and lighten up, okay?*

Five steps. Her mind screamed. Do something before you melt into a puddle on the sidewalk.

Emma turned her back to him and posed with one hand on her hip. She shifted her weight so that her back side moved provocatively in her tight jeans. She watched Tate's face over her shoulder.

Six steps. Emma smiled, "Tell me Tate, is it still a pretty little tail or what?"

Seven steps. Was that a growl?

Emma turned to face him, let go of the bag at her side

and lifted her arms. Her feet left the ground as Tate pulled her into his embrace. Emma wrapped her arms tightly around his neck, closed her eyes and held on. Her fingers found their way to the hair at the nape of their own, weaving themselves into the soft dark strands. She pushed closer, and breathed in the scent of him as she silently wanted herself. *It won't work Emma.*

Watching Emma turn and shake her backside had really gotten to Tate. *Get over it Echo. You can't have it.* Forcing his legs to move, Tate took another step and then another until he reached her. He wrapped her in a tight, and long overdue, hug. Tate forced himself to stop thinking, allowing himself to let go and just feel for the first time in a very long time. Emma in his arms. Her body pressed flush against his. Tate closed his eyes and savored the sweet citrusy smell of her hair, the feel of her breasts pushed tight against his chest. Silently he cursed. *Tate, what have you gotten yourself into? You know you'll never keep her.*

Letting her body slide against his, Tate set Emma down and playfully swatted her backside. "You know damn well that your ass is just as gorgeous as it ever was, just like you knew that I wouldn't be able to look away when you turned around and shook it for me."

Emma laughed and turned toward the SUV with her bag in tow. Reaching out, Tate took her arm and pulled her around to face him. "Em, it's good to see you, but don't thing for even a minute that I'm not going to ask you some very personal questions about why you're here."

Opening the rear door of the SUV, Tate tossed Emma's bag inside and watched her closely as she silently slid into the passenger seat and pulled the door closed.

Tate hopped in and started the vehicle, then turned to face her. "So, where to?"

"Your house, of course. Surely you don't expect your ex-wife to stay in a hotel. What would your mother say if she found out that you were that unaccommodating?"

Tate felt the rumble of a growl in his chest again, or maybe it was a groan. Tate pressed the gas pedal and the SUV eased out, moving smoothly into the light traffic around the terminal.

Tate shook his head and frowned, "Emma, I don't know what's going on or why exactly you're here, but you can bet the farm that I intend to find out."

She ignored the comment.

He slid her a sideways glance, "You know that you're welcome to stay at my house, even better, stay in my bed, but I need to understand what the rules are, and what exactly you're up to."

CHAPTER 20

"Look dad, it's not that hard to use. You just put the coordinates from the geocaching website into the GPS, and then you follow it to the site and voila! The treasure's yours!" Tapping one manicured finger on the small screen, Jewel Mabry continued, "This thing will get you within a couple of feet of the cache, and then you use the clues that are on the website to find it."

Jewel handed the GPS over to her sixty-year-old dad, who turned it over in his large, work-roughened hand while looking at the small screen. Today was his birthday, the handheld GPS a gift from Jules.

"You're going to like this better than your metal detector, because you'll always find the treasure—no more quarters or bottle caps," she promised.

Smiling at his daughter's excitement and knowing that she'd given him this blasted thing hoping he would get out and walk more, Walter patted Jewel's hand. Since his heart attack last spring, she'd come up with any number of ways to keep him busy. First it was that damned treadmill, then the metal detector, and now this.

"Okay, Jules, I'll give it a try. Help me find some of those treasure numbers on the computer and get them loaded in before you leave. I might just take me a drive this afternoon and see what I find."

After helping her father load several nearby cache coordinates into his new GPS, Jewel kissed him goodbye on the cheek. "Don't be out late Dad, remember we're all having dinner for your birthday over at The Rib Shack, seven sharp."

"Don't you worry none about that baby girl." Walter smiled, "I won't be one minute late. I can smell the wood smoke and that sweet sauce now."

Laughing at her father's excitement over the dinner, Jewel stepped off the porch and walked to her car. She turned and blew him a kiss, "Love you, Daddy!"

Reaching down, Walt placed on hand on the head of a German Shepherd standing on the porch next to him, and then waved, "Love you too sweetie." He continued to wave as he watched his only child back her car from the drive. When he could no longer see her car on the dirt road leading to his farm, Walt turned and went inside, the dog followed on his heels.

Walt sat in a faded tan recliner and examined his new birthday gift for a minute before exchanging it for the television remote. Reaching over and rubbing the dog's head, he said, "Maybe tomorrow, King. Yeah, we'll go looking for treasure tomorrow. Judge Judy is coming on in a few minutes and I can't miss that old broad making a fool out of somebody today."

Placing one large paw on his master's knee, the dog stared at him with rich brown eyes.

"Don't you worry none, King, I'll be sure to bring you home some nice juicy rib bones." Walt continued to rub the dog's head, laughing at Kings excited tail wag. "That is, if I don't gnaw the bones myself. Been way too long since I had some barbeque ribs. Jewel makes sure everything in this house is green or made of cardboard. She says 'fiber is good for you, Dad.' Hah! You're lucky she hasn't took away your favorite treats King, or caught us down at the diner on meatloaf day."

Walt shook his head and flipped through the channels to find his show. What would Jules come up with next? "Here we go, King. All rise!" Letting out a sharp bark the dog lay down at his master's feet and rested his large head on his paws.

CHAPTER 21

Sliding out of the SUV, Emma looked appreciatively at Tate's home for a minute. Sitting off the road a few hundred feet, the house was small but neat on the outside with a large front yard that had been recently mowed. Sighing, Emma thought that the only thing missing here was a couple kids playing in the yard and a pretty woman in the doorway to welcome him home. Her mind traveled further down that path, and she wondered how long it would be before Tate added the missing pieces to his small town life.

This could have been your fairytale, her heart screamed. He begged you to come with him.

As Tate rounded the front of the SUV, Emma pasted a smile on her face and moved aside so that he could pull the rear door open.

Grabbing Emma by the hand, Tate pulled her up the driveway and the steps leading to the front door. He pushed the door open and stepped back so that she could enter before him.

"You always leave your door unlocked?" Emma asked.

Tate moved past her in the small entryway and turned down the hallway with her bag in tow. "Yeah well you never know when an ex-wife or two might show up needing a place to stay."

Emma followed Tate into a small bedroom at the end of the hallway and watched him put her bag down just inside the door. He pointed across the hall to a nearby bathroom.

"I've got a couple steaks in the fridge, so make yourself at home while I get the grill started. And Em, just so you don't think I've forgotten, first we eat, and then we talk."

Emma stood and listened to the sound of his boots on the smooth wooden floor faded. She hoisted her bag onto the bed and unzipped it, staring at her clothes for a moment before she sank down on the edge of the bed. *Emma, what are you going here?* She wondered.

In her heart, she admitted the answer to her question; after so long, his voice on the phone just wasn't enough. She had to see him, smell him, touch him and have him touch her back. His needing her help gave her an excuse to come to Pine Ridge and the impulse overwhelmed her common sense. In that weak moment she'd hopped a plane to South Dakota; so now what? This would be self-torture at its best and at the worst? Emotional suicide for sure. She buried her face in her hands. Emma you are a fool. *Do you have any idea how hard it's going to be to walk away from his this time?*

Emma pushed herself up from the bed and crossed the hall to the bathroom. Bending at the white pedestal sink, she splashed her face with cool water, trying to calm her nervous energy. *You are here to help find a killer and that is all, Emma. That is all. Now, go help Tate with dinner and pretend everything is fine.*

Emma stopped in the hallway when she reached the door to Tate's bedroom. She couldn't resist a peek. The room was large with double windows facing the back yard. The late day sun drifted across the room through open blinds. A king-sized bed dominated the room. In one corner, an overstuffed arm chair sat near a window and was flanked by a small table.

The smooth wooden surface of the table was dust free and topped with an open book that lay face down saving Tate's place in the text. Emma crossed to the table and picked up a gold framed photo sitting next to the book, a photo of them taken shortly after their wedding. With one finger she traced a line across the faces of the laughing couple in the photo. Tate stood behind her, his arms locked around her waist while she twisted back and looked up at him. *We were happy then*. She thought.

"Reminds you of better days, huh?"

Emma was startled to see Tate standing in the doorway, his shoulder resting against the frame of the door. "Why didn't we try harder Em?"

He'd changed from his uniform and the soft t-shirt that he wore clung to the hard muscles of his chest and arms. Sucking in a quick breath, Emma bent and retuned the photo to its place. Emma stepped around him into the hallway and said, "Let's just put everything on hold for one night, okay? No blame, no questions; just two old friends catching up, alright?"

Tate trailed behind her as they went down the hall, "Sure Em—one night, and then you're going to tell me what the hell you're really doing in Pine Ridge."

Hours later, the sun had given up its last rays to make way for the night, and the occasional glow of a firefly flittered in the air, blinking a florescent yellow-green. Puffy trails of smoke escaped the grill and snuck skyward in the soft breeze until they disappeared into the darkness.

"The steaks were great," Emma sighed.

Tate twisted the top off a bottle of beer and handed it to Emma. "Glad you liked them."

Emma relaxed in the darkness and watched as the sky filled with stars. "It's so peaceful here. No traffic, no sirens. And the stars! You can see so many more here than I can in the city." She wanted to talk about the murders, but knew that tomorrow would be soon enough to talk about the case and all the other things that she'd tried to forget. But for tonight, she wanted to rest and drink in the peace and comfort she felt just knowing that Tate was close by.

Emma felt the warmth from Tate's hand on her brow as he pushed a stray hair from her face. He was so close she could feel him breathing. She wanted him to kiss her, but would it be the first step down the same disappointing path that they'd already traveled? She felt Tate lean away and took the opportunity to stand, gathering their empty plates. "It's been a long day. I think I'll turn in now."

In the darkness, Tate's smile faded. He'd almost kissed her, almost crossed that point of no return and it had taken what? A few hours and one steak? Seriously? He had zero self-control with that woman around and the fact that she was so close already had him wound in knots.

He'd done his best to keep the conversation light, asking about friends and co-workers in the city and she'd done the same. Polite conversation. It was the only safe space they could share at this point. That and work, of course.

Tomorrow Tate was sure Emma's FBI façade would be back in place and she would once again become the tough, insightful investigator that he knew she was. She'd always been that good, but tonight he'd seen the longing on her face, a tiny crack in her armor. She wanted him as badly as he wanted her. But then what? Checkmate. When they were together he could never entertain the thought of losing her, and in the end, he'd lost her anyway.

CHAPTER 22

Gavin dodged a large grey-white granite boulder, and then went up and over the next one in his path. This formation of rocks marked the northern boundary to the Pine Ridge Reservation and although the dirt road leading to the site was rutty and dusty, it was easily accessible.

Following the directions on his GPS, Gavin whistled under his breath. "This is my kind of place. Serious cachers only, private and four finds in the last two weeks."

Just across the road was public land and beyond that, the Badlands National Park. Gavin squatted down and felt under a rock ledge until his gloved hand made contact with the cache. Still whistling under his breath, he popped the top off a yellow margarine tub.

Looking into the cache, he frowned, "Same old crap here. Let's add something interesting to the mix." He reached into his jacket pocket and pulled out his token. Gavin caressed the token for a moment before dropping it into the container. "Perfect. Just need to get the show set up and we're all done here, Gav."

He slid the cache back into its hiding spot and pushed some gravel around the ledge making sure the cache was hidden from view. Stepping back, Gavin surveyed the area looking for a good place to set up his camera. "Hmm, no trees."

Securing the mini-cam between two boulders, Gavin angled the camera upward, certain that the device could do its job in spite of the bad location. He pulled his jacket off and tied it around his waist before stepped back through the rocks. At the edge of the site, he slid down a small incline to the unpaved road below where he stood with his hands on his hips and lifted his face up to catch the fading rays of a South Dakota sun. Soaking up the warmth, he whispered, "Won't be long now, Mama. You'll see. They'll come."

Still whistling, Gavin crossed the road and slipped into a thicket of pine and cedar growing on the other side. He's set up camp a few hundred feet into the fragrant woods, and thanks to the state contract he was working, he knew that his Wi-Fi signal at camp would be perfect.

Earlier in the day, he'd entered the Badlands National Park, hidden his car in a remote area, and then hiked through the woods to this particular spot. He wouldn't be missed and presumed lost, because he'd registered as a day use guest, meaning that he would leave before the park closed. He'd never understood why the park system thought it was important to register guests coming into the park, but didn't count them going out. *Hell, anyone could be in these woods or in the park after normal hours.*

Gavin knew that it might take a day or two before anyone came looking for this cache, but he didn't care, time was one of many things that he had. Every year, thousands of tourists came to see the Black Hills and to visit either the State Parks or national Parks that were carved into thousands of acres across South Dakota. There had been Indians living in the Dakotas for hundreds of years and the state was rich with history; for the nature lovers the scenery was breathtaking.

Stepping into his primitive camp and sitting on the pine-padded ground, Gavin opened his laptop to check the view from his camera. As the cache sight popped up on his screen, he smiled. "So far, so good, Gav my man. Now you wait."

The woods were shadowed and cool under the tall trees and Gavin already noticed a drop in temperature as evening approached. He'd dressed in layers when he'd left this morning, knowing that the extra clothes would assure that he could survive a cold night or two in the woods. Gavin untied the lightweight jacket from around his waist and pushed his arms through the sleeves, and pulled the zipper up.

Need to get a fire going. It's going to be a cold night. He gathered fallen branches and twigs, and then stacked the wood in the middle of a small circle outlined by rocks. Stuffing dried pine needles around the wood, Gavin pulled a box of matches from his pocket and lit the needles; standing back and watching the flames grow.

Taking a seat near the fire, his back resting against a tall pine, Gavin fished a granola bar from his backpack and tore the wrapper open. He loved the anonymity and solitude of being alone in the woods at night. He smiled and leaned forward to toss another branch on the small campfire, watching as sparks formed a blinking ribbon of color rising into the darkness. The occasional pop of burning wood provided the night's only sounds.

Fantastic night for a campout, Gav. Crossing his legs in front of him, Gavin watched the flames change from red to yellow and the shadows dance on the ground while he finished his granola.

Gavin pulled his sleeping bag free from his backpack and rolled it out close to the fire. He pushed pine needles into a pile and slid them under one end of the bag. "Ahh, nature's pillow."

Gavin tugged the cover up and zipped the sleeping back half way. He turned away from the mystical rhythm of the dancing flames and closed his eyes. He willed his body to relax and sleep. Slowly rocking himself, Gavin tried to ignore the gut-deep ached that called to him. He needed someone to take the damned coin or, at the very least, he needed to watch one of his recordings.

"No movies tonight, Gav. Gotta save battery power for now. It won't be long." The tension inside him had built faster than ever before and he knew of only one way to relieve it. Feeling helpless, he thought of his mother and how she'd always read to him until he fell asleep as a child.

"She'd know how to fix this," he whispered, remembering how she would hold him, and rock him when he'd been scared.

Turning to his back, Gavin propped his hands behind his head and stared at the night sky peeking through the trees. Stars twinkled at him from miles above the earth, and he cursed the shiny token that he'd placed in the cache hours before. The coin intrigued the cachers, forcing them to take it, but they weren't the only ones enslaved to the coin. He was a prisoner as well.

CHAPTER 23

Emma woke the following morning to the rich smell of coffee followed by the 'get your butt up' aroma of frying bacon. Stretching, she burrowed a little deeper into the covers and thought of the mornings when she and Tate were married. Tate was always up before sunrise. He loved the freshness of a new day, when the grass was still damp with the nights' dew he'd sneak out of the house and jog in the park near their apartment, returning to shower and start breakfast before she'd ever opened an eye.

Her face heating, Emma thought of the mornings when she'd only pretended to be asleep, and some of the more creative and down-right erotic ways that Tate had employed to wake her up.

Wrong way to start the day Emma, she groaned. Tossing the covers aside, she slid from the bed and slipped into the bathroom for a quick shower.

Tate heard the shower running and frowned. Secretly he'd hoped that Emma would need a little help getting up this morning, and he knew just the right way to wake that woman up. He clenched his jaw. *Don't go there Echo, you know how the story ends so there's no reason to read the book again.*

His mood soured, thinking of all the things he wanted but couldn't have. Tate turned back to the waiting pan of scrambled eggs and reached for a spoon. He shoveled eggs onto two plates just as Emma entered the kitchen. God, she looked amazing. Her hair, damp from the shower hung loosely down her back. Emma wasn't one of those women who took hours to dress, she wore just a touch of make-up and today she had only a shimmer of something creamy peach on her lips, making her look young and fresh.

She smiled, "I see you still like to start your day with a full plate."

Nodding, Tate handed her a steaming plate of bacon and eggs, and gestured to the table where two glasses of orange juice stood waiting.

"Mmmm," Emma closed her eyes and groaned in pleasure when she took a bite of the eggs.

Watching Emma's face while she ate, Tate felt his mood lighten at her pleasure. That was his Emma. She gave herself completely whether making love or, well, eating eggs.

His Em. Wrong!

Emma looked at Tate, the smile on his face was teasing. "What? It's not like I get this kind of breakfast every day. Most of the time, it's a granola bar and some juice. I'm in Utopia right now, so I would appreciate it if you didn't make fun of me!"

Tate's laugh rumbled deep in his chest before erupting in the small room. "Emma Echo, I have missed watching you eat. Among other things," his voice trailed.

Her smile was mischievous and infectious, so they sat there grinning at each other like kids in a candy store window. A call on Tate's cell broke the spell. He stepped into the living room to take the call. When Tate returned to the kitchen, Emma had finished her breakfast and was rinsing her plate. The moment was gone.

She turned and smiled at him, "So what's on the agenda today, Chief Echo?"

Leaning on the counter, Tate reached to turn off the coffee maker. "I want to start with a full review of both the Parker and Babcock cases. Chances are you'll be able to pull out some detail that Martin and I missed. Then we'll make a run by both the murder sites if you want. I will need to let Martin know that we're going out to the lake since the Babcock case if officially his."

"Give me a sec to grab my computer and my jacket and then I'll be ready to go," Emma said.

Arriving at the courthouse, Tate steered Emma into his office without stopping for his usual good morning chat with the desk clerk on duty. He switched the coffee maker on and opened the blinds to allow the morning sun to streak into the room. He wasn't ready to explain who Emma was, or answer any questions about why she was here, and he certainly didn't want to field any questions about their relationship, past or present. What he couldn't avoid were the curious looks that several members of the force tossed his way.

"Let them wonder about it for a while," he muttered.

Studying a large area map hanging behind Tate's desk, Emma pointed to the push pins marking the map and asked, "These are the kill sites?"

Nodding, Tate moved to his desk where he pulled out the folders on both cases, sliding them across the desk to her. Emma already knew about the geographical differences in the two cases, but the map allowed her to see just how far apart the murders had occurred, and gave her a good feel for the size of Shannon County. Taking a seat across from Tate, she opened the Parker file and read the reports from the ME's office, and those completed by his own department.

Next she moved to the photos in the file, laying them out in time-line order on Tate's desk.

Filling two mugs with coffee, Tate plunked one down on the corner of his desk for Emma before taking his seat. Watching Emma's face as she read, Tate was reminded of just how beautiful she was. Right now, her face was scrunched up in concentration as her eyes scanned the pictures on his desk. She had pulled her silky hair out of the way and it hung over one shoulder, the dark strands begging him to reach out and touch their softness. Tate wondered how he'd ever had the courage to walk away from her, job or no job, family or no family. Wouldn't having her in his life any way that he could have been better that what he had now? Sighing, Tate knew the answer to that. He could have stayed, hell, he'd wanted to stay, but what would the compromise have cost in the long run? Reassuring himself that he'd done the right thing was easy. It was better to walk away while he could still love her than to stay and watch their dreams die one day at a time.

Sitting back in her chair, Emma picked up the waiting cup of coffee and took a sip before she spoke. "Okay, so tell me what you know, and then tell me what you think."

Tate smiled at her. Emma had always been direct and to the point when she was working, and some things just don't change.

"Well, so far, the geographical profile has been relatively consistent with both murders taking place in Shannon County, and both victims were at the lake the day that they were killed."

Holding up her hand to stop Tate, Emma asked, "So you think that there are, or will be, more victims? If that's the case, then you really should invite the Bureau in since we both know that they have resources that you simply don't have access to."

Shoving a hand through his dark hair, Tate stared at Emma, his jaw twitched with frustration. "Em, you know I can't do that yet. I have a job to do and the city of Pine Ridge is depending on me to catch this guy. I can't go crying to the Bureau every time I have a problem that I don't have the proper resources for, it's not the way that small towns handle crime." He signed, "That's why I called you. I need your expertise with the profile, and then I intend to catch this guy before he has a chance to kill again."

"Okay, we'll table this for now. We've established that he likes Shannon County and the lake. So far that's our only common denominator. What else?"

Relaxing a little, Tate sat back, "Well the victimology is off. First a woman, then a male child, with no personal or direct links between Parker and Babcock. By the way, we are certain that it's a *he,* the ME confirmed penetration the usual way and they also found traces of pre-ejaculate fluid." Nodding, Emma reached for her cup again as Tate continued, "The killer's signature is consistent in both cases. Same markings, rape, kill cuts..." pointing to the photo of Saralyn's bound hands, Tate added, "Same red cording used on both vics and both had Ketamine in their systems. Our working theory is that the killer uses the drug to subdue the victims."

"So does the ME think that there was a condom used and that's why there was no full ejaculate present?"

Tate loved it when Emma went into research mode. Her tenacious memory, coupled with her unrelenting pursuit of the facts, had proven her to be an unstoppable force when working a case. He needed that ability now, he needed Emma. "Nope, there was nothing to indicate that a condom was used. Appears the guy just wouldn't, or couldn't, finish what he started."

Emma looked thoughtful, "Well, there could be a medical problem causing his inability to ejaculate, you know, like a blocked duct or something. Also, there are studies supporting the idea that a known percentage of rapists have an ejaculatory dysfunction. That's not saying that they are impotent. Most of the case studies present evidence that the perpetrator needed something more before they were able to complete the act."

"You mean like torturing their vic while raping them?" Tate asked.

"Exactly. In some cases they need to torture in order to feel in control or powerful. Other studies cite that a small percentage need help with their fantasy, and make the vic dress up or act in a manner that fulfills their need. Any sign of that with these cases?"

Tate rocked back in his desk chair. "None. And with the Parker kill, he had the time to do that if he'd wanted to. Another common link with the two cases is that both Parker and Babcock had been geocaching while they were at the lake."

"Geocaching?" Emma asked. "I read something about that recently. Some kind of treasure hunting, right?"

Tate turned to his computer and entered the geocaching web address into the browser. He turned the screen so that both he and Emma could see it. "Says here that it's a growing sport both in the U.S. and internationally. Currently the site claims that they have something like a million participants worldwide. The Babcock's gave me their log in information for the website and I've played around with it. Seems that you go into the site and enter the zip code for the area that you want to search in and it gives you a list of caches and their coordinates. Then you enter the coordinates into a GPS and it leads you to the cache. Once you find it, you go back on this website and log your find. That way the cache owner knows how many people have found his hiding spot, and you can track the number of caches that you've found as well.

Emma scanned the screen, "You do any research on the caches at the lake?"

Nodding, Tate replied, "Yep, and there's ten hidden just in the lake park and over fifty in the county. Seems that State parks are a popular place to hide them. There's one hidden at the site where the Babcock boy was killed. Martin and I went out and took a look at it the same day that the boy's parents told us about it. Basically, it was a plastic container covered in camo tape and hidden under some rocks." Logging into the website, Tate accessed the Babcock's' cache log and entered the coordinates for the cache. "The Babcock's didn't log the find, and there was no record of Reva and Saralyn finding this one either. Several others logged this particular cache, so the Babcock's weren't the first to find it, but I do think that they were the last. We took the container into evidence, but didn't pull any prints from it, other than all the members of the Babcock family."

"So you think that if the killer touched it, that he wore gloves? This guy can't just sit in the woods and wait for someone to show up. There's something that we're missing. I want to see one of these caches."

Tate nodded, "Also, if this is the same cache that Parker found the day she was murdered, then she didn't have time to log the find before he got her. Reva doesn't have a computer and said that Saralyn always logged their finds. She gave us their log in ID but didn't know the password. The county lab pulled a report for me from Parker's computer using a back door entry into the caching site and didn't find any record of this particular cache. The Sheriff drove Reva out to the Babcock scene and she didn't recall looking for, or finding any cache there."

"Maybe he monitors more than one site. Let's take a ride out to the scene, okay?"

Tate glanced at the clock on his desk. "How about we grab some lunch at the diner then drive out to the lake? We can stop by Parker's house on the way back."

"Lunch does sound good. Since we're going out to the lake, let's enter some of the geocaching coordinates into the GPS on my phone and take a little hike. I'd like to have a better understanding of how this works, and there's no better way than doing it myself."

Ten minutes later, Tate and Emma had loaded three waypoints into Emma's phone. Tate had just strapped on his service revolver when the door to his office opened and Martin stepped in. Noticing Emma seated at Tate's desk, martin flushed with embarrassment, "Sorry Tate, I didn't know you had a visitor. I'll come back."

Tate smiled as he snapped the leather safety strap over the top of his gun, "Come on in, Martin. I'd like you to meet someone. Martin, this is SSA Emma Gag-Echo." Turning to face Emma, he continued, "Emma, this old geezer is Martin Crawley, the Sheriff of Shannon County."

Martin grasped Emma's extended hand in welcome.

Emma spoke first, "Sheriff Crawley, it's nice to meet you. Tate told me about you and the two cases that you and he are working on. In fact, we were just about to grab some lunch and then go take a look at the kill sites."

Tate bit back a smile. Martin still held Emma's hand, and it was easy to see that he was totally charmed with the beautiful ex-Mrs. Echo. "Why don't you join us for lunch, Martin?"

Seeming to recall that he was in Tate's office, and that Tate was in the room, Martin dropped Emma's hand and turned to face his friend. "Huh? Oh, sorry. I already had my lunch, but thanks anyways. I just stopped by to see if you'd heard back from the FBI and it appears that you not only heard from them, but have one visiting."

Sliding the strap of her bag over one shoulder, Emma shared, "I'm here unofficially Sheriff Crawley, but I do hope that I can help in some way."

"Please call me Martin. I sure hope that you can help us catch this bast--," Martin's face reddened "Excuse me ma'am, I mean, I sure hope you can help us catch this UnSub, too."

Surprised by Martin's self-consciousness, Emma tried but couldn't stop the laugh that bubbled up. Tate didn't even try to stifle his own laughter. "Martin." Emma emphasized the sheriff's first name, "I am certainly going to do everything possible to see that the *bastard* who did this is caught." It was obvious to Emma that Martin had been raised a gentleman. After six years in the FBI, Emma couldn't imagine that there was a dirty word that she hadn't heard, yet this sweet man was embarrassed to have almost said 'bastard' in her presence. She liked him already.

Clapping Martin on the shoulder, Tate said, "Stop by the house when you finish your shift, if you have time, and we'll bring you up to speed on anything we might discover. Like Em said, we're going to visit the murder scene out at the lake, and while we're there we're going to do a little geocaching ourselves. We don't know for sure that it relates to the murders, but at this point, we don't know that it doesn't either."

Saying his goodbyes, martin agreed to stop by Tate's on his way home.

CHAPTER 24

Walt Mabry climbed into his ten-year-old pickup right behind King. The German Shepherd had been a gift from his late wife more than five years ago, and Walt rarely went anywhere without him. Pushing a button on the door, Walt lowered the passenger side window half way because King liked to ride with his nose to the wind

In the seat between man and beast lay his old hat, some sunscreen, and his new birthday gift. Talking to the dog as much as to himself, Walt laughed, "Damned if Jules wasn't right. This GPS thing is more fun that the metal detector and it sure beats that treadmill she was always trying to get me on. People walking on those things and never going anywhere makes about as much sense as all those folks who run in the park when nobody's chasing 'em." Walt reached over and ruffled the dog's ears. "Whatever happened to the good old days when you worked all day, came home to a meal cooked by a pretty woman, and watched some TV until bedtime, huh King?" Barking his agreement, King turned back to the half-open window.

Walt turned his truck onto the bumpy unpaved road, and then reached over to steady his new GPS on the dash, watching the directions as he drove. Avoiding the deep ruts and potholes the size of a small pond, Walt kept one eye on the GPS and one on King as he bounced on the bench seat of the old truck. A couple miles farther down the dirt road, Walt pulled over to the road's edge in what looked like the closest place to get out and walk toward the treasure. Opening the truck door, he grabbed his hat.

"To hell with that sun stuff, huh, King? Jules is too fussy. Took after her mama, she did." Jules insisted that he take sunscreen along anytime he was planning to be outside, lecturing him about skin cancer and anything else she thought he didn't know. "Both my girls fussed too much, King. Good thing you're a single guy." Plucking the GPS from the dash, Walt said, Come on King. Let's go find us some treasure!"

With a yip, the dog jumped from the truck seat and followed as Walt let the way. Not bothering with a leash, Walt knew that King would stay at his side and together they climbed the small incline to the rocks above. Following the cursor on his GPS, Walt circled one large boulder then another. The climb was steep, but not impossible. Small beads of sweat popped out on his face and Walt stopped to wipe them with his sleeve before bending over to look under the rocks for the hidden cache.

Fifty yards away, Gavin's computer beeped and the familiar pop up appeared on the screen. "What the hell? All I can see are shoes and rocks! This shit cannot be happening again."

Closing his computer and grabbing his jacket, Gavin sprinted to the edge of the thick piney woods. Sucking in deep breaths of pine infused spring air, he willed his heart to slow. *It's all good Gav...don't freak out. Maybe you'll get a chance to fix the cam.*

Standing under the cover of the tall trees lining the roadway, he watched while an old man and a large dog climbed slowly toward the cache. The old man stopped to mop the sweat from his face and Gavin wondered if he was going to make it up the hill.

"Damn, I didn't think anyone would come after this one so soon. I should have checked that camera this morning."

Gavin's need was so great that he'd almost convinced himself that coin or no coin, this cacher would be the one, but he knew that he couldn't make that choice. Only the coin could decide. It would choose and Gavin would take great pleasure in bowing to its choice. Moving closer to the road's edge Gavin squatted hoping to avoid detection. He continued to watch the old man.

Sensing or maybe smelling another human in the area, the large dog raised its head. Gavin swore that the beast looked right at him. Peeking through the thick underbrush growing at the base of the trees, he whispered, "Dog's going to be a problem, Gav."

Pulling a faded yellow margarine container from its hiding place, Walt sat down on the large rock that the cache had been hidden under and popped the top to see what was hidden inside. So far, he'd found two other caches this morning and he'd taken something from them both. From the first cache he'd taken a pick that was topped with an American flag, and from the second cache he'd taken a one dollar lottery ticket. The tiny flag now waved from the sun visor in his truck and the lottery ticket had been a two dollar winner.

"Let's see what we can find in this one, King. Hope it's another lottery ticket, 'cause I'm on a roll. Hell, I might even go buy me one of those Powerball tickets when we head home. I feel lucky!"

The old man sat there for what Gavin calculated to be a full ten minutes before he finally snapped the top back on the cache, and slid it under the rocks. Gavin saw the man slide his hand into his pants pocket, and then motion for the dog to follow him back down the hill.

"Old man, without my computer, I can't tell if you took my coin or not, but you sure as hell found my cache and that's good enough for me." Shaking his head, Gavin pushed away the urge to act on his own thoughts rather than waiting to honor his pact with the coin. *You know you can't do it unless he took the token, Gav.* He reminded himself. *What would Mama say? There's only one way to find out what you need to know without your computer, so suck it up and go talk to the old guy. Just stay away from that big ass dog.*

Walt made his way down the hill, and then opened the truck door and waited for King to jump in the truck. Walt knew that it wouldn't be too many more years before the dog was going to need a boost to make the seat. Hell, maybe he'd buy a car, something that they could both get in and out of with less trouble than the truck. Slamming the truck door closed, Walt walked to the rear of the vehicle.

Still hidden, Gavin watched until the old man loaded the dog in the truck. Instead of getting in himself, the old guy made his way to the rear of the truck and unzipped his pants to take a leak.

Now, that was a lucky break. Show time, Gav.

As the old guy zipped up, Gavin stepped out of the woods, GPS in hand. Calling a friendly hello, he walked toward the man.

Looking up, Walt replied, "Hey there, you looking for that cache thing?"

Gavin stepped closer, peered at his GPS and replied, "Yeah, that's what I'm doing. You find it?"

Walt leaned against his truck and slid one hand into his pants pocket. "I sure did and look what I took from it."

Pulling his hand free from his pocket, the old man extended his arm and his hand opened to reveal the coin. Just the sight of his coin resting in the old man's calloused hand caused Gavin's blood to rush from his heart to his head, where it pounded like the native drums that had beat on this land for hundreds of years.

Turning his head toward the cache site, Gavin hoped to hide the raw exuberance that coursed through him, but more than that, he frantically searched for a way to stall the old man while he repositioned his camera.

You need that video!

Knowing that the window of opportunity was small, and that the old man would most likely leave before he could move the camera, Gavin gave up the idea as another one took its place. Squatting to tie his shoe, Gavin said, "Pretty cool, hope you left something for me to find."

The old man never stopped talking long enough to realize that Gavin had moved uncomfortably close, or that he now held a large rock in one hand. Gavin shoved him against the truck, pinning him against the warm metal. Inside the truck's cab, the dog barked and clawed at the window, a vain attempt to help his master. As the rock in Gavin's hand cracked with a sickening thud against Walt's skull, he staggered, his body sliding down to the rocky sand on the side of the road.

Struggling to remain conscious, Walt looked up at the younger man with unfocused eyes, "Why?"

Not bothering to answer Walt's question, Gavin reached into his jacket pocket and pulled out a hypodermic needle, and a strand of red cording. He pushed the needle into Walt's neck with the quiet efficiency of an emergency room doctor, and then slid the empty hypo back into his pocket. Walt struggled to stand, but Gavin easily pushed him back down and began to wrap the cording around his wrists. "Just wait for it, old man. You'll be in K heaven any second now, and once your there, you won't even care that you're not coming back."

Securing Walt's hands in front of him, Gavin stepped back to give the drug time to work. He'd given the old guy a pretty good dose, so he knew that it wouldn't take but a couple minutes for the potent drug to take its full effect. Jogging quickly up the hill, Gavin made his way to the mini-can and positioned it so that he should have a clear view of Walt leaning against the side of his truck.

Noticing that the small green light on the device was not illuminated, Gavin cursed, "Fuck. This just gets richer by the minute." Giving the camera a good thump, he kicked it when the light still didn't come on. The camera rolled down the incline, landing a few feet from Walt. Making his way back down the hill, Gavin stopped, scooped up the camera and carried it back with him.

Squatting in front of the man, Gavin reached out and pulled one half-closed eyelid up. "Feels good, doesn't it old man? I knew you'd like it." Pulling a scalpel from his pocket and removing the protective covering, Gavin stared at Walt, knowing that it was time.

Struggling to speak, his words slurred, Walt looked up with unfocused eyes, "My chest..." His face was red and twisted with pain.

Realizing what was happening, Gavin cursed and grabbed Walt by the shoulders, and shook him. "Damn it, old man! Don't you dare die! Only I can decide when you go—do you hear me!"

Minutes later, Gavin stepped over the crumpled body of Walt Mabry. Pausing, he stared at the ground and Walt's blood seeping into the dirt, already forming a dark pool on the dry sand. The dog in the cab of the truck hadn't given up his mission to save his master. He frantically barked and pawed at the window before growling low and watching Gavin walk across the dirt road and out of sight.

CHAPTER 25

Now back to where she and Tate had parked the SUV, Emma pulled her hair out of its ponytail. "Well I can certainly see why people like geocaching! Looking for hidden treasure is a lot of fun, but I do wonder if it really had anything to do with the cases, or if it's just a coincidence."

"Yeah, I know what you mean," Tate agreed. "I have a hard time believing that there's some guy out there stalking cache sites and waiting for a victim to show up, but you will have to admit that it's pretty strange that Justin's body was found at the same place his family cached at earlier in the day."

Emma nodded her agreement, "I'd like to talk to everyone who logged that site in the last week, to see if they found anything strange about the site or if they noticed anyone lurking. I plan to call the geocaching website owner and officially ask him to disclose the names and any other info available on those who logged that site."

"Good place to start, Em. It's getting pretty late, how about we save the Parker house for tomorrow morning?"

"Sounds good to me. I could really use a shower. I also want to do some research on the killer's signature. Maybe there are similar cases on file."

Tate turned the SUV onto the tree-lined road leading from the lake. "Home it is. While you're getting a shower, I'll make a couple of my world famous grilled cheese sandwiches."

Quickly turning away to stare out the passenger side window, Emma wondered if Tate realized that he'd made it sound like they were going to *their* home, not his home where she was just a temporary visitor. *Damn it, Emma, it could have been your home if you weren't so stubborn. It still could be, but how long would that door be open?*

Breathing deeply, she wasn't surprised when a heavy sigh pushed past her lips. This was no time for self-recrimination. She was here to help solve the murders, as a friend, nothing more.

Sensing Emma's mood change, Tate glanced at her but didn't speak. Her forehead, creased with worry wrinkles, gave the rest of her face a solemn and sad look. *Wonder what she's thinking about.*

"Something bothering you Em? Emma?" No answer. "Earth to Emma!"

Snapping back to the present, Emma turned to face Tate, her cheeks warm and a few shades brighter than normal. "Sorry, what were you saying?"

"Just wondering why you look so solemn. What's on that busy mind of yours?"

Emma gave him a sad half-smile, and then frowned. "Nothing important, just daydreaming." She looked away, afraid that Tate would somehow see through her eyes and into her heart, where he would find little pieces of the well-built armor she'd worked so hard to construct around her heart slipping away from the fragile organ.

The rest of the short ride home was made in silence. Emma continued to stare out the side window, and Tate couldn't help but notice that she'd twisted a strand of her long hair around one finger. A sign he recognized only too well. His Em was either thinking really hard, worried, or upset. Hell, maybe she was all three. *You've got to stop thinking of her as your Em. Been there, done that already.* But in his heart Tate knew that she would always be his Em.

Tate stopped to grab the mail from his mailbox before pulling the SUV into the detached garage and parking it next to his personal car. Reaching for the door handle, Emma was surprised when Tate reached out and grabbed her arm, pulling her around to face him.

Brushing Emma's cheek with the backs of his fingers, Tate whispered, "Don't worry Em. Everything will work out just the way it's supposed to, whether we like the end result or not."

With the strangest urge to cry, Emma leaned into his hand. She tried to smile but her lips quivered and refused to cooperate. Instead they convinced her head to help them by turning into his caressing hand, where those same traitorous lips proceeded to press soft kisses against Tate's palm.

Tate didn't know what exactly was happening here, but he really didn't care either. Emma was here and she was kissing his hand. Hell, he'd take a crumb if that's all there was in the bread box. He'd spent too much time thinking about the past or the future, and for now, all he wanted to think about was this minute...just this one minute, nothing more.

Tate clasped his free hand behind Emma's neck and pulled her forward until their lips met. The kiss was tentative at first, as if they were testing the water of an unknown river. A moan escaped Emma's lips, and that soft little sound pushed Tate over the proverbial edge. No more testing the water, he didn't care how deep the river was. Pushing his tongue past Emma's lips and into the sweetest warmth he'd ever known, Tate deepened the kiss, pulling Emma tightly against him.

Emma's brain screamed, *STOP*, but her heart and body weren't listening. Instead, she moved closer, her hands climbing the hard planes of his chest. She grasped his shirt collar and pulled him closer. Opening her mouth wider, Emma accepted all that Tate offered. Slowly, logic seeped like a dripping faucet from her brain to her heart.

Tate felt the change and pulled back far enough to look into Emma's eyes. He saw what he already knew. It was just a kiss, nothing had changed for them. But what a kiss it was!

"I...I shouldn't have let you kiss me. Can we just forg..."

Cutting her off, Tate said, "Emma, first of all, it wasn't just me kissing you, I seem to recall someone else's tongue bouncing around in my mouth. Second of all, you can forget anything that you want. As for me, I doubt that I could forget it if I want to, and third, well hell, I don't want to forget."

Sensing that he'd pushed the subject about as far as he could without totally ruining the moment; Tate jerked the door handle open and stepped out of the SUV. He went out the side door of the garage and into the back door of his house, leaving Emma to find her way in. They could both use a little space.

Watching Tate's back as he left the garage, Emma groaned. *What are you doing Emma? You know better than to kiss him. Damn it!*

Emma stepped out of the vehicle and stomped into the house. She slipped past the kitchen and turned down the hall to the bedroom where she gathered a clean pair of jeans, a faded t-shirt, and some underwear. She stepped into the small bathroom and reached behind the curtain to turn the water on. Emma stripped, letting her clothes drop to the cool tile floor. Standing under the hot spray, she scrubbed at her lips, trying to wash away the kiss she'd shared with Tate, but all that did was remind her of it more. The familiarity of his soft lips, the way that he tilted his head, and most of off, the way his hand felt on the back of her neck, massaging, caressing, loving...

"Stop it! Stop it right now, Emma Gage-Echo. All you're doing is sensationalizing the whole thing. It was just a kiss; you didn't even like it that much." Enunciating the last words through gritted teeth, Emma reached to turn the shower off knowing that she'd just told herself a big fat lie.

CHAPTER 26

Sitting on the front porch smoking a cigarette, Martin cursed when his cell phone rang. Glancing at the caller ID and seeing that it was dispatch, he groaned, "There go your plans for a quiet night at home making love to your wife, Martin."

Martin stepped into the house and grabbed his gun, keys and hat. "Sorry, Hun," he called to his wife, "but I've got to make a run over to Walt Mabry's. Jewel called the station a little bit ago and said that she hadn't been able to get a hold of Walt all day."

Drying her hands on a faded kitchen towel, Barbara stepped out of the dining room, a worried frown creasing her forehead. "I sure hope Walt is okay, it would just kill Jewel if something happened to her daddy."

Nodding, Martin said, "Jewel's been out of town for two days and she's worried that Walt may have had another heart attack and not been able to get to the phone. It's not like hi to ignore Jewel when she calls."

He kissed Barb's forehead. "This shouldn't take long and I'll be back in time to watch that movie you rented."

Wrapping her arms around his thick middle, Barbara gave Martin a tight squeeze, resting her head on his shoulder for a minute.

Twenty minutes later, dust flew behind the patrol car as Martin turned into Walt's driveway and sped up to the house. *Hmm, no lights on and no truck in the driveway.* Martin got out of the cruiser and grabbed his police issue flashlight. Cautiously, he stepped up onto the porch and knocked on the door. No answer.

Shining his flashlight through the living room window, Martin thought, *Everything looks in order, at least in this part of the house.* Martin made his way around to the back and then reached above the door frame for the spare key that Jewel had said was there when she called the station. Unlocking the door, Martin entered the house. If Walt was here, he didn't want to scare him or have Walt pull out that old shotgun of his, thinking that there was an intruder.

"Walt. It's Martin Crawley. You here buddy?" Not getting a response, Martin moved from room to room, searching the small frame house for Walt or signs of trouble. Turning his flashlight off, martin flipped the kitchen light on, illuminating the small room. No mess, no signs of foul play, nothing out of the ordinary. *Maybe Walt was just out later than usual and Jewel missed him when she called,* he thought. Leaving the house the same way he'd entered, Martin locked the door behind him. He hit redial on his cell, and had the dispatcher forward his call to Jewel. He assured her that he would come back by the house in the morning to check on Walt, and she promised to call if she heard from her daddy. Martin backed out of the drive and drove home to his waiting wife.

The following morning, Martin kissed Barb goodbye on the porch, and took the travel mug of hot coffee that she always had ready for him. He waved goodbye. Since he hadn't heard from Jewel the night before, or this morning, he planned to stop by Walt's on his way to the station. Taking a slug from his cup, Martin thought, *Maybe I'll get a refill from*

Walt. Anything is better than that watery coffee that comes from the machine in the break room. He was sure that Walt would have turned up by now.

Pulling into the driveway, Martin was shocked to see that Walt's truck still wasn't parked in its usual spot. He got out, knocked on the back door, and then let himself in when he didn't get an answer. Martin was greeted by the same empty house that he'd walked through the night before. Not a thing had been disturbed. Back in the cruiser, Martin took a small dirt road that went down the east side of Walt's property thinking that Walt might be down at the old barn. Martin hadn't thought to check the barn last night, but now he was worried. It wasn't like Walt to be out all night. There must be something wrong.

After a quick trip down to the barn turned up nothing, Martin drove back the way that he'd come. As he was leaving, Martin called the station and asked Kevin Walker, the desk clerk on duty, if there had been any reports during the night regarding Walt Mabry. There hadn't. "Kevin, do me a favor and call the county hospital to see if by some chance Walt was admitted. Check for John Does as well, since he may not have been able to ID himself. I sure hope we find him because I don't want to have to call Jewel and tell her that her daddy is still missing."

Martin was disappointed when he arrived at the courthouse a few minutes later and found that there had been no record of Walt being admitted to the hospital and there were no John Doe's either. He couldn't put it off any longer, he had to call Jewel. Martin closed his office door and dialed Walt's daughter.

CHAPTER 27

Emma silently slid into a chair across from Tate at the small table in his kitchen. The tension of last night's encounter in the garage had lessened, but still stood like a wall between them.

Looking over the morning paper, Tate announced, "Your plate is in the oven." He let the newspaper slide back up so that the morning news blocked his grin. Emma had barely spoken ten words to him last night after the kiss, but he could almost see her mind as she analyzed and compartmentalized the events that occurred in the garage.

You're getting to her Echo, just don't push her too hard or you know she'll run.

Emma opened the oven door and pulled a plate rounded with bacon and eggs out of the warm box. She slid it onto a placemat, then sat down and picked up her fork. She paused and cleared her throat, "Tate, I know that it was little awkward last night, but can't we just move forward? We need to push everything but the case to the back burner for now, and find the killer. What do you say?"

Letting the paper drop a few inches, Tate's grey eyes bored into Emma's blue ones from across the table, one corner of his mouth lifted in a half smile. "Whatever you think SSA Gage-Echo."

Emma breathed a sigh of relief that Tate wasn't going to make a big deal about the kiss. *That God for that.* She had been afraid that one little kiss was going to be a dark cloud hanging over them for the rest of her trip. Pushing another fork of eggs into her mouth, she smiled back at Tate. "Glad to see that you know who's in charge, Chief Echo," she teased. Emma's smile broadened and then she giggled.

Tate stared at her in puzzled surprise, "What the heck is so funny? You losing it?"

Emma continued to laugh, pushing back from the table and hugging her middle as the giggle turned into a full out laugh. "Oh, Tate, I just realized that you're now *Chief Echo.* Chief, as in Indian Chief!"

Catching her meaning, Tate scowled at Emma from across the table. Laying the paper aside, he warned, "Do not laugh at my heritage Em. The chief will have to order you to be staked to the bed and tortured if you keep it up, and I promise you *will* enjoy the particular torture that I have in mind."

Forcing the laughter down, Emma giggled, "Bet the guys at the office give you hell with that one, huh?"

Standing to rinse his plate, Tate replied, "Not to my face they don't, but I've heard rumors. So what's on the agenda for today, Em? You still want to see the Parker scene?"

"Yeah, I do. Also, last night I got a call back from the owner of the geocaching website. He agreed to email me all the information for people that logged finds in the county for the last two months. I already downloaded the finds that the Babcock family logged that were within a fifty mile radius of Pine Ridge. I want to cross reference the logs and see if anything pops."

Tate leaned against the counter with his coffee cup in hand. "Sounds like a solid plan. Did he say how long it would take? I left a message with that damn place two days ago and they haven't even returned my call, what'd you say to get them on the ball?"

"Simple, F-B-I. That got me to the right person in about three seconds." Emma continued, "Mr. CEO promised he would get the information to me no later than one this afternoon. Seems it's a pretty easy process for the website owner. I also thought that we should check the Bureau database to see if there have been any similar cases recorded at other State or National parks. As many parks as there are spread across the country, what's to say that this guy is specific to South Dakota?"

Tate frowned as he rinsed his cup and placed it into the dishwasher, "Well, I did check the systems that I have access to, no results, but I was searching based on the killer's signature. Now that we are aware of the park's link and the geocaching, maybe we could come up with some tighter search parameters."

Stepping around Tate, Emma rinsed her plate and placed it neatly into the dishwasher next to his. "Let me grab my computer and I'll be ready." Emma headed down the hallway to Tate's office where she'd left her computer to charge. As she pushed the office door open, she heard Tate's cell phone ring in the background.

Tate glanced at the caller ID and answered, "Good morning Sheriff. What's up with County?"

"Tate, it seems that Walt Mabry is missing. Jewel called yesterday and said that she hadn't been able to get a hold of him all day. I went by the house and his truck is gone, and it appears that King is with him where he is. No sign of foul play at the house."

Cutting in, Tate asked, "Slow down a minute, have you checked the hospitals? We all know that Walt has a weak heart, maybe he drove himself over and got checked in."

"Negative on that," Martin replied. "We checked the hospitals, both here and in White River with no Walt and no John Does either. Jewel says that she talked to him the night before last and he was fine."

Tate looked up as Emma entered the room with her bag in hand. Holding up one finger, he signaled that it would be just a minute.

"With Walt's known medical condition, I think you should go ahead and issue a Silver Alert. Walt isn't exactly over the hill, but he is considered elderly. Did Jewel say what Walt had planned for the day yesterday?"

"She didn't know if he had any plans or not, but she did mention that she'd given him a hand-held GPS for his birthday this week and thought that he might be out looking for geocaches. Said she gave it to him hoping that he'd get out and walk more. Jewel's real worried that he got out and had an attack and wasn't able to get back into town. I didn't want to scare Jewel more than she already is, so I didn't mention the possible link in the Parker and Babcock murders to geocaching, but I'm real worried about Walt. I've got patrols on the county roads now, hoping that we can locate him. I was hoping that you could add a couple cars to help broaden the search."

Tate agreed, "That goes without saying. I was just about to run by the Parker house and let Em have a look at the scene, but we'll table that for now. I'll call dispatch and have all available patrols assigned to the search. Keep the line open so that they can reach out to coordinate directions with you. Em and I will join the search as well. Any particular place you want us to start?"

After coordinating an initial search area with Martin, Tate hung up and turned to see Emma staring at the newspaper he'd left on the table, a frown creased her brow. "Did you see the picture in today's paper?" Folding the paper backward on the crease, she handed it to him.

"Son of a bitch!" Tate cursed. Page three featured a picture of him and Emma embracing when he'd picked her up at the airport. "Police Chief cavorts with an unknown woman while killer runs free." Slamming the paper down on the table, Tate seethed. "I'm going to kill him for this."

Emma placed one hand on Tate's forearm. "Kill who? Why does something like this warrant a picture in the paper?"

Disgust lacing his voice, Tate fumed, "Em, we have a leak in either my department or Martin's. Someone has been feeing information on the murders to the locals, stirring up trouble and hard feelings, and generally trying to make a fool out of me. Martin thinks he knows who it is, and has someone from internal affairs assigned as the guy's partner. He's hoping to flush out some proof but that's not helping me solve these murders or maintain my standing as police chief. Damn it."

"So why does someone want to undermine your position or the investigation?"

"Pretty simple, Em, I'd been gone a few years and one of Martin's guys, Pete Green, had a son that just graduated top of his class from the academy. Seems he thought his son was a shoo-in for the job, and then I got in the way. I can't believe the Mayor hasn't called yet. Rumor around town, according to a waitress over at the diner, is that I must have been a lousy FBI agent if I had to come back to Pine Ridge to get a job."

"So you didn't tell them about our divorce or that the Bureau practically begged you to stay, and even offered you a transfer if you'd take it?"

"I didn't tell them anything, Em. It's none of their damned business why I moved back home. Right now, I have more important things to worry about. Walt Mabry has been missing since yesterday. His daughter just gave him a GPS for his birthday, and thinks he may have gone caching and had a heart attack. Since we were at the lake yesterday and know where some of the caches are out there, Martin asked that we patrol that particular area in case Walt went there to search for caches too. He's got all available staff searching the back roads and I'm adding city staff to the search as well."

Emma nodded, "Damn, we've got to find this guy before we have a third murder on our hands. But I also want to do a little reputation saving starting today. What time does the next shift come in? Or better yet, since the department is so small, what do you think about calling them all in for a briefing first thing tomorrow morning?" Pulling the strap of her computer bag up over one shoulder, Emma moved to the back door without waiting for Tate to answer.

On the drive in to the courthouse, Emma outlined her plan, "I want to call a press conference, admit that I'm with the FBI, and that I'm here on an unofficial basis as a personal favor to you. Then I want to share the tentative profile information that I have on the UnSub with the staff so that they have a better idea about what we're dealing with. That should shut the leak up for a while and give the press something new to focus on."

Tate nodded his agreement and flipped the blinker on as he turned the SUB into the courthouse parking lot.

Taking Emma by the hand, Tate led her up the courthouse steps and into the dispatch area of the department offices. Stopping at the reception desk, Tate introduced Emma to Julie Barton. "Julie, I need all staff here thirty minutes before shifts in the morning for a meeting with SSA Gage-Echo. She will be facilitating the meeting to go over a tentative profile for our killer. Martin will be pulling in all available sheriffs' department staff as well, so schedule a room that's large enough to hold us all please."

"Sure thing, Chief. You want me to put a memo out to the staff now? If I hurry I can get them in mailboxes before the shift change so that everyone is notified."

Tate smiled, Perfect. I appreciate you help. I've got a couple things to handle here, and then we're going out to help the county with the search for Walt, call on my cell if I'm needed."

"You go it, and we'll hold the fort down here, Chief."

Driving through the White's Lake property, Tate and Emma kept an eye out for Walt's truck. If he had come to the lake, he hadn't bothered to check in at the front desk. Giving up their search inside the lodge proper, they began to cruise the many back roads just outside the lodge's boundaries.

Turning the SUB onto an unmarked road, Tate slowed the vehicle, dodging the sandy ruts made by other travelers. "This is the area where we find most of the locals who slip down to fish the lake. Keep an eye out for anyone. If Walt came this way, chances are someone else was out here too."

"Why wouldn't Walt, or anyone else for that matter, just come through the gate into the lake area?" Emma continued to scan the countryside. "I mean, the roads are better, they have goats and the pier."

"The locals slip in because they don't think it's right that they have to pay to fish the lake. Martin gets an occasional call for someone fishing without paying, but for the most part, the locals fish the lower edge of the lake and stay as far away from the lodge and campgrounds as possible. If he was fishing, Walt would have come this way, he's local to the core and probably wouldn't go through the lodge. I sure hope to hell he came to fish and not to search for damned geocaches."

Emma kept her eyes trained out the passenger side window. "So the sheriff's department just turns a blind eye to illegal fishing out here? That doesn't seem right."

"Yeah, I know it's not by the book, but it's different here. We stay inside the law on most things, but you have to take into consideration the demographics here. Small town, large Native American population, hell, some of the Natives consider it their birth right to fish any lake in the county or to hunt in any unpopulated area, whether it's actually on the Reservation or not. There's also a lot of poverty here, you don't notice it so much inside town, but in the rural areas people are hurting. Jobs are scarce and money's tight for a lot of people. When you look at all the bad things going on in the world today, catching a few fish from a lake as big as this one just doesn't seem to be much of a crime."

"Stop, Tate! Back up."

"What did you see?" Tate asked, braking.

"Not positive, but I caught a flash of something through the trees about twenty feet back. Could have been a truck or car. God, I hope it's him."

Tate maneuvered the SUV backward to the spot Emma indicated, and parked as far off the road as he could before getting out. "Come on, let's go see who's down there."

A narrow trail, not much more than the flattening of grass, ran down to where the truck was parked. Emma and Tate followed it down.

Before reaching the parked vehicle, Tate called out,

"Hello! This is Police Chief Echo, I need to talk to you for a minute."

Tate and Emma watched as two heads popped up over the hood of the truck. Kids.

The two boys stepped around the truck to face Tate and Emma. The taller of the two explained, "We was just fishing, Chief. Nothing wrong with that."

Recognizing both boys, Tate asked, "You see anyone else out here, Cory?"

Shaking his head, the shorter boy said, "Naw, we ain't seen anyone else out here today."

Emma asked, "What time did you boys get here?"

The older of the two answered. "About sun up ma'am. Been right here all day."

"Look boys, Walt Mabry's been missing since yesterday. Half the town's searching for him. You're sure you haven't seen him out here?" Tate asked.

"We're sure, Chief. I know Mr. Mabry real good, and I'd remember if I'd seen him because he always has his dog in the truck with him."

"Either of you have a cell phone?" Tate asked.

Cory replied, "I do, Chief, and I've even got a little signal out here."

"That's good, if you see Walt, King, or even a truck that looks like Walt's, you call 911." Tate and Emma jogged back to the road, the sun hung low in the spring sky, it's orange and red rays fading fast. Time was not on their side.

Slapping a hand against the steering wheel, Tate swore. "Damn it, Walt! Where are you?" Turning the SUV around on the narrow road, Tate punched Martin's number on his cell.

"Crawley here. You find something Tate?"

"No sign of Walt out here. We're headed back to town and should be at the courthouse in about thirty minutes, I take it that none of the volunteers had any luck either?"

Martin replied, "Nothing. It's like he just disappeared off the face of the earth. Curtis Weston over at the pine Ridge Daily did get a hot line set up, and he's got some guys from the VFW manning the phones. So far, there have been over twenty calls but they were all dead ends."

Tate disconnected the call and turned to Emma. He shook his head. "Nothing."

Martin pulled his staff and those on loan from the city back to town as night fell, knowing that they would need their rest so that the search could resume the following day. As the men and women came into the station, Martin could see the exhaustion and frustration that lined their faces. Tate and Emma arrived back at the courthouse in time to hear Martin giving directions to his officers and the volunteers for the following morning.

Speaking loudly, Martin said, "The sheriff's department thanks each one of you for helping with the search today. We will officially resume the search in the morning, just after daylight. Any of you volunteers that are available to help, can come in and we will assign you a search area for the day. I know that we all hoped to find Walt today, and I won't lie to you about it, each hour that passes lessens our chance of finding him safe and well, but we will not give up."

When the last of the volunteers left the courthouse, Tate approached Martin, "Looks bad Martin. Your team find anything at Walt's house that might help?"

Looking much older than his fifty four years, Martin shook his head, "Not a damn thing. Nothing in the house was disturbed, and even though they dusted for prints there wasn't anything there that we couldn't account for. Looks like Walt just went out for the day and didn't come home. Only thing we know for sure is that wherever Walt is, King is with him. Jewel got into town this morning and she stayed at the house all day in case Walt came in. Every time I talked to her today, she was a little more upset. She knows that the longer he's missing, the worse it is, and there's not a damn thing I can do to make it right for her."

Tate clamped a hand on Martin's shoulder, silently supporting his friend.

Stepping up to Tate's side, Emma said, "Everyone knows that with each passing hour the chances are lessened that we'll find Walt, and sad as that is, if it was his time, then I hope he did have a heart attack. That would be a much better way to go than what would happen if he ran into our caching killer."

Martin grimly nodded, "I've got to stop over at Walt's and talk to Jewel before I call it a night. Barb has been over there most of the keeping her company and she plans to stay the night if Jewel will let her. I'll see you tomorrow for the briefing."

Twenty minutes later, martin pulled his patrol car into Walt's driveway and parked behind Barbara's car.

Before he could know, Jewel threw the door open, her eyes red with tears but hopeful. "Did you find my dad? Please tell me that you did."

Shaking his head, Martin cleared his throat before saying, "Nothing yet, Jewel. Let's go inside and I'll bring you up to speed on the search effort."

Barbara stood a few feet behind Jewel in the doorway and she silently moved forward, wrapping an arm around

Jewel and leading her to the dining room table before disappearing into the kitchen.

Taking a seat across from jewel, Martin softly said, "We've called off the search for toni…"

Jewel jumped up from her chair. "How could you! How could you just stop looking for him? He's out there somewhere and he's probably sick or hurt! You can't just leave him out there all night, he could die!" Storming to the back door of the house, she continued, "I've got to go find him, I can't just sit here and wait."

Martin rushed to the young woman's side and wrapped an arm around her heaving shoulders. He pleaded, "Come on, Jewel, have a seat and let's talk about this for a minute."

Shrugging his arm off her shoulder, Jewel turned on him, her eyes wild with rage and fear, "NO! I've got to find my dad. I've got to…"

Taking her firmly by the shoulders, Martin forced her eyes to his, "Look at e. We start the search back at first light. There's nothing that we can do in the dark with a search area as large as this one. I can't risk the lives of the volunteers by sending them out like that, Jewel."

Jewel melted, collapsing in a heap on the floor, her head buried in her hands. Tear-filled eyes looked up at Martin. Sucking in a deep, steadying breath, she said, "I'm sorry Sheriff, it's just," her voice cracked, and she whispered, "He's my daddy."

Martin took Jewel's hands in his own larger ones and pulled her to her feet, and wrapped her in a tight hug, "I know, sweetie, I know." Looking over Jewel's head at Barb standing in the kitchen doorway, martin nodded before scooping Jewel up in his arms like a child and following Barb down the hall to the bedroom.

After a quick stop by the diner, Tate and Emma sat on the deck eating burgers from a greasy brown paper bag and watching night fall in the tiny back yard.

Pulling a paper napkin out of her lap, Emma wiped her mouth. "A penny for your thoughts, Chief Echo."

"My thoughts probably aren't worth a penny tonight, Em. Hell, Walt is missing, probably dead. Martin's got his hands full trying to keep Jewel from falling apart and somewhere out there...somewhere out there, there's a killer that I haven't found. I'm tired of chasing my tail on this case, I want him. I want him now."

Stuffing her trash into the now empty paper bag, Emma stood, "We'll find him, it'll happen. There's not much more that we can do tonight, and I haven't had a chance to check my computer all day. I'm going to grab a quick shower, then take a look at the information that the geocaching site owner promised me."

Reaching out as she passed, Tate grabbed her free hand and brought it to his lips, pressing a soft kiss to her palm before letting go. He heard the patio door open then close, and knew that she'd walked away. Muttering, he said, "Just let it go Echo. The wall's up and there's no way around it... yet."

CHAPTER 28

Tate and Emma arrived at the courthouse thirty minutes before the morning shift change. Volunteers lined the hallway in the reception area, waiting for their assigned search areas and hoping to find the missing Walt. Nodding to several of the locals, Tate steered Emma toward the briefing room that Julie had reserved for the meeting. For the first time since she'd arrived. Em was in full FBI mode: dark slacks, matching jacket, and her FBI photo badge clipped at her waist. Her long hair was pulled back and clipped, the mahogany strands hung sleekly down her slender back. Tate opened the door and followed her into the briefing room. Standing back, he watched her walk to the front of the room. "It's your show, Em," he whispered.

Stepping up to the podium at the front of the room, Emma waited while officers from the sheriff's department and the city police department filed in and took seats. Taking a deep breath she scanned the room, looking for the Greens.

"Good morning. My name is Emma Gage-Echo and my title is Supervisory Special Agent with the Federal Bureau of Investigation." Making eye contact with the two men that she'd pegged as Pete and Chad Green, she continued, "I'm guessing that some of you saw my picture in yesterday's paper, but that is not what I'm here to discuss today. I am currently working with Chief Echo and Sheriff Crawley regarding the murders occurring in and around Pine ridge. My official position with the FBI is Criminal profiler, and I want to share my tentative impressions of the killer with you."

Moving to the front of the podium, she leaned against the metal edge of a desk. "Before I begin, are there any questions?" a hand at the back of the room went up. *Here we go,* Emma thought. Pointing to the fiftyish man, Emma asked, "Officer Green, right? You have a question?" Others in the room turned to look at Pete Green, waiting to see what he would say.

Nervously pushing his glasses up on the bridge of his nose, Pete Green stammered, "Yeah, I have questions. What are you and the new chief doing to find this killer?" His voice dripped with insinuation. "Hugging in the airport?"

Emma smiled. *So that's how it is. I'll play along.* Standing, she let her eyes drift around the room, making eye contact with several officers in the crowd before landing on Pete. "Ah, so hugging in the airport is offensive to you, Officer Green?"

Snickers sounded around the room.

"Just to please you, Officer Green," Emma said, "I'm going to address your question. However, it has absolutely nothing to do with the issue of finding a killer. I'm not sure how the citizens of Pine Ridge welcome friends, but where I come from it's perfectly acceptable to hug a friend in the airport, or anywhere else. I'm also certain that you caught my name. Emma Gage-ECHO, surely you occasionally hug your wife, Officer Green, assuming that you've got one that is."

Outright laughter from the crowd this time.

From his post near the door, Tate leaned against the frame, a faint smile on his lips. *Green doesn't know what he's stepped in messing with Em, but you can bet there's going to be some of it left on his shoes.* He thought.

Noticing that Pete's face was now the appropriate shade of red, Emma resumed. "Does anyone else have questions before I continue?" She noted the shaking of heads. "Perfect. Now we can move to the real reason that you've been called here today. Our killer." Glancing at Tate, she winked, and he nodded his approval.

"The UnSub is a male, confirmed by the ME reports. He's in his early to mid-thirties, and can clearly be classified as a sociopath. His primary hunting ground so far, has been in and around the White's Lake Resort, and there is a strong indication that he frequents geocaching sites. This UnSub is going to look normal in every way. He's friendly and most likely maintains normal relationships with friends and family." Emma stopped speaking when a hand went up at the front of the room. "Yes?"

A well-built man in a dark brown sheriff's department uniform stood. "Yes ma'am. You say this psychopath hunts at the lake, but Ms. Parker was killed in town, wouldn't that change your profile?"

Smiling, Emma explained, "That's a good question. First of all, Mr. Parker had been at the lake, and it has been confirmed that she was searching for geocaches the day of her death, as was the Babcock child. It's possible that the UnSub followed her back into town. Secondly, this UnSub is not a psychopath, but rather a sociopath. He's meticulous in planning these kills, brings his own kill kit, and leaves no clues. While both the sociopath and the psychopath are extremely violent, a psychopath would behave more erratically, killing without a specific plan, and would most likely leave clues that so far haven't been left for us Does that answer your questions, office?"

At the officer's smiling nod, Emma continued to field questions around the room. Knowing that she had this group under control, Tate stepped out and motioned for Martin to follow. Stepping into the central lobby, Tate and Martin greeted the search volunteers and passed out assigned grids for the day's search.

"Tate, have you seen today's paper?" Martin asked.

"Nope, but tell me that there's not another picture of my personal life in there today, please."

"Nothing on you. The front page has a picture of Walt and King, and says that Jewel is offering a five thousand dollar reward for information about her daddy."

Whistling through his teeth, Tate said, "That should get the phone lines hopping. Maybe we'll get a good lead with that much money on the table."

"I'm sure we'll get calls, but I don't think the news is going to be good when we find Walt. It's been too long and if he was able, I know Walt would have called Jewel by now. There's no way that he would have kept King out this long without going home to feed him either. Curtis has volunteers manning the phones in four hour shifts today, and he's going to call either you or me with any leads. Him and Walt have been friends since high school, when they both played on the football team. This is tearing him up."

Tate watched Emma walk into the room, her FBI personal still in place. Motioning Tate over, she waited by the door. "I need to talk to you for a minute before we go out on the search team. I think it would be best if Martin joined us too."

"Sure. Let's go into my office." Crossing the hallway, Emma, Tate and Martin closed the door behind them. "So what's up?" Martin asked. "You find something, Miss Emma?"

"Maybe. You know that I got the logs from the geocaching web owner showing everyone who logged caches at the site where Babcock was murdered, all of Parker's finds, except the one for the day she was murdered, and a detailed roster of finds on the other caches in the county. I did a cross reference and didn't find that Parker and Babcock had been to any similar cache sites, but a lot of other people had found the same caches as both Parker and Babcock."

Confused, Martin asked, "So what's the link?"

"Well, seeing how many people found the same caches as both our victims got me thinking. How does he decide who to kill? Clearly he hasn't killed everyone who found these caches, so why Parker, why Babcock? I don't think he sits in the woods and waits for a victim that fits a certain profile to come along either. He hasn't been consistent enough with his victim selection for that to be a consideration at this point."

"Maybe it was just random," Martin reasoned.

Emma smiled, but discarded the idea. "Could be Sheriff, but I don't think so. This guy is too meticulous in his planning and I can't believe that he would plan so well for the actual kill, and then wait for a random victim. What did catch my eye is that each time one of our victims found a cache, they took something from it, leaving something of theirs in return. That's one of the rules of the game. They log what they took and what they left in its place. What if our killer is selecting his victims not by the site, but by what they take from the cache?"

Tate sat on the corner of his desk. "That's a little bit of a reach, Em. How would he know who took what? He's killing the same day that they find the cache and neither Parker nor Babcock logged their find from that day, so he can't be going into the site after they find it and then tracking them down somehow."

Nodding, Emma agreed. "I know it's a long shot, but I think it's worth looking into. Did you ask the Babcock's or Parker's friend what they took? If not, then I really think we should, to rule this theory out if nothing else."

Martin spoke up, "Sounds a little far-fetched to me too, but I can't see what it'd hurt to ask them about it, Tate. Why don't you and Emma run by the diner on your way out to search for Walt and talk to Reva, and I'll call the Babcock's. I'll call you if I get anything from them before I go out on my search."

CHAPTER 29

Fingering the coin in his hand, Gavin traced the etched design. He tossed his backpack into the rented car he'd left hidden in the park, and then slid behind the wheel. "I had it made for you mama, it's our coin. I'll be home soon. Maybe we'll go buy a big house with a yellow kitchen, just the way you like it."

Pulling the car into gear, he drove through the park without stopping at the gate. Gavin knew that his mother wasn't going to leave the center, and that there would be no big house with a yellow kitchen, but talking to her and planning a future for them both was something that he needed to do. Driving through Pine Ridge, Gavin smiled when he saw all the cars and people in front of the courthouse.

"The search is on," he snorted. Not slowing, Gavin followed the road out of town to where it intersected with I-30. He pulled into the parking lot of a lonely motel and walked inside.

Tate and Emma entered the diner and took a seat at the bar. The place was packed and Reva hurriedly took orders. Seeing them at the counter, she smiled and nodded to let them know it would be a minute. Tate returned the nod.

"Coffee to go Em?"

Before Emma could answer, Reva stepped up to the counter with her pad in hand and asked, "What'll it be Chief? I see you've got company today. Waffles for two?"

Shaking his head no, Tate replied, "Reva, I'd like you to meet Emma Gage-Echo. Emma's here unofficially as a member of the FBI to help with the murder cases."

"Nice to meet you, Reva," Emma said. "I'm sorry about your friend. It's hard to lose someone you care about. I know you're busy, but I have a couple questions that I'm hoping you can help with."

"Thank you ma'am, Reva replied, "Me and Saralyn were good friends, and it does hurt." Noticing Burt glare through the open window above the counter, Reva hesitated. "The diner's real busy today and I got customers waiting, so if you could wait about ten minutes until the other waitress comes in, I'll be able to take a break and talk to you. That okay?"

Emma nodded, "Sure it is. We'll take two black coffees while we wait, please."

Tate and Emma took their coffees and went to the only open table at the back of the diner to wait for Reva. Fifteen minutes later, Reva slid into a chair across from Tate. "Burt says I've got ten minutes, so what questions did you have for me?"

"Reva," Emma asked, "on the day that Saralyn was murdered, you and she were caching out at the lake, right?"

Reva nodded, "Yeah, but I already told Tate that."

"I know you already told Tate, but I was wondering if you recall taking anything from the cache that you found that day?"

"Well sure, we always took something and Saralyn kept a little plastic bag in her car of things that we could put in ourselves. Nothing much, just things like pencils, erasers or stickers. She was a teacher, you know."

Tate interrupted, "So do you recall what you took that day?"

Wiping her hands on a faded apron tied at her waist, Reva frowned, "Well, I think it was some kind of coin. Saralyn kept it because she was going to log it." Her voice breaking, Reva continued, "I guess she never got the chance."

Patting the other woman's arm, Emma asked, "Can you describe it Reva? What color was it? How big it was, anything that you can think of might be helpful."

Reva grabbed a napkin from a spring loaded silver box in the middle of the table and wiped her nose, and then shoved the napkin into her apron pocket. "Well, I carried it to the car and Saralyn said I should keep it, but I made her take it so she could log the find better. It was a little bit bigger than a fifty cent piece because it fit in the palm of my hand good, but it was gold colored, not silver like a fifty cent coin would be. Both sides had engraving, one side had a picture of something and the other side had words, but I don't recall what they were." Glancing at her watch, Reva looked over her shoulder, checking to see if Burt was watching the clock too.

Following her gaze, Tate stood and reached into his pocket, tossing a five on the table. "Think about it, and if you recall anything about that coin, give me a call. You've got my car with my cell number, right?"

Standing, Reva reached for the empty coffee cups and nodded, "I will, and it was real nice to meet you, ma'am."

Turning to leave, Tate and Emma weaved their way through the diner to the door, and stepped out. Emma spoke,

"So what do you make of that? Is she afraid of her boss or what?"

Tate laughed as they walked to the SUV, "She's definitely not afraid of Burt. He's scary looking, but that's about as far as it goes. Inside, he's a softy. He wouldn't have said anything if she'd sat there for an hour, but he doesn't like any customer waiting for very long, and Reva doesn't like to upset him, or miss out on any tips, I'd imagine. Tight as money is around here, she needs every nickel she earns."

Tate had just turned out of the diner parking lot when his cell phone rang. Seeing that it was Martin, he pulled off to the side of the road to take the call. "Echo here."

"Tate, I just got a call from a deputy on patrol, they found Walt and it's bad. Can you meet me out on County Road 2214? That's the road that borders the Res on the northern end."

"On my way. Who found him?"

"Gary Barnes found him while doing regular patrol. My team only runs that road a couple times a week because it's so isolated. I already told him to hold off calling the coroner until we take a look, and he's working to secure the scene now."

Tate pulled the SUB into gear and eased back onto the road, glancing at Emma as he continued to listen to Martin.

"Barnes says that it appears to be a homicide, and from the description, it's the same bastard."

Tate hung up and quickly relayed the details to Emma. There was little traffic in town today with almost everyone out looking for Walt or in the diner. Slowing, Tate turned the SUV onto County Road 2214 and picked up speed on the bumpy dirt track bordering the Reservation. A tunnel of white dust billowed behind the SUB, announcing his arrival.

Fifteen minutes later, Martin, Tate and Emma stood looking down at Walt Mabry's crumpled and mutilated body. Squatting in front of the dead man, Tate blurted, "Why an old man? He's changed victim types three times now. We've got to find this son of a bitch."

Moving to stand at the end of Walt's truck, Emma turned to face Tate when a flash of light caught her eye. Moving slowly so as not to disturb anything at the scene, Emma quickly slid a latex glove on, stooped and picked up a piece of glass from the ground. Turning, she held it up to the sunlight. "Take a look at this."

"What is it?" Tate made his way to where Emma stood at the end of the truck.

"Not sure, but it looks like a camera lens. How would something like that get out here?" Tate also slid on a glove and took the broken glass from Emma, holding it between his thumb and forefinger to examine it.

"Tag and bag it. We'll let the guys at County lab tell us exactly what it is, and then determine if it has any significance." Turning to Martin he continued, "Any sign of the dog, Martin? I'm wondering how someone got close enough to hurt Walt with King around."

"Yeah, he was in the cab of the truck. Poor old guy was pretty dehydrated. I had Barnes pull him out the passenger side and give him some water, and then load him into the patrol car with the air running. Wore out as he was, me and Barnes still had hell putting him in the car. He kept trying to get to Walt."

Emma peered into the passenger side window without touching the truck, and said, "Looks like he did a fair job of trying to get out, the windows are covered with what I can only assume is dried dog slobber, and there are deep scratches on the top of both doors and below the rear window. Too bad he wasn't able to get free."

Martin pointed down the road at a cloud of dust. "Looks like the CSU team is on the way in." He turned to his deputy. "Barnes, take King over to Doc Wells and have him checked out. Go ahead and ask him to keep King until Jewel can be notified. Be sure you go in the back way so that the whole town doesn't know yet."

Gesturing to the three member crime team climbing out of their van, Martin continued. "We'll finish up here and then I'll come back to the office before I call Jewel. Do not let this leak out to anyone before I get a chance to call Jewel in and tell her."

"You got it, Sheriff." The young deputy replied.

One of the men from the Crime Scene Unit called out, "Sheriff, I'm pretty sure I have the murder weapon here. Take a look at this rock. There's dried blood, hair and some other matter stuck to it. Seems consistent with Walt's head wound."

Martin nodded, "Bag it up and get it over to the lab, Jeff. Try to keep it intact and dry."

Martin watched the second man of the team as he dusted the outside of the truck for prints. "Be sure you get the inside of the truck too, matt." Without looking away from his work, the man acknowledged Martin's request with a nod.

Opening the passenger side of the truck, Tate surveyed the cab for anything out of place, and then bent to take a look under the seat. That's when he noticed the hand-held GPS device laying in the floor. Pulling a paper napkin from his pocket, Tate retrieved the GPS with one hand, and hit the power button with the gloved hand to preserve any evidence. Dead. Turning, he motioned the female member of the crime team over and said, "Once you three are through dusting this, I'd like to see what data is entered on it. Battery's dead now, but I think it may give us some insight as to what Walt was doing out here."

The tech nodded, pulled a large bag out, and slid the device inside. With a black Sharpie, she noted the time, date, and place on a square paper label attached to the bag, and then moved to place the item in her holding box.

Drawing Martin outside the yellow crime scene tape, and away from the primary evidence bearing area, Tate pointed to the cruiser's tire prints in the dirt road. "Walt went missing three days ago and we had rain four days ago, and while it may have washed away any foot or shoe prints, tire tracks usually leave a rut in dirt roads like this, especially after a rain." He pointed to the deep ruts behind Walt's truck. "I don't see any ruts or tire prints leading up to this point, or going forward, other than those made by Walt's truck. Doesn't appear that anyone has traveled this road from the time that Walt stopped here, until Barnes came through on rounds."

Martin looked closer, "Yeah, I would agree with that. So you're saying that our killer walked up here? Hell, it's at least four miles from the highway to this point. If he was walking, maybe Walt passed him, or even stopped to give him a ride."

Tate scanned the other side of the road, staring into the dense copse of trees. "Or just maybe, he was already here. The question would now be, did he come down from the hills on Reservation property, or did he cross the road from the woods over there?"

"Why either one?" Martin puzzled. This is just about the most isolated spot on the Reservation. I can't imagine what someone would have had to maneuver around if they came across the Res land, and they would have had to cross on foot because no car could make it through all the rocks and ravines."

Tate moved toward the road. "I agree. It's more likely that our UnSub came from these woods."

Motioning Emma over, they all crossed the dirt road, and pushed their way into the thick pine and cedar trees on the opposite side of the road from where Walt's body still lay. Their footsteps were silenced by the thick covering of pine needles carpeting the ground.

Martin was the first to speak as they entered the woods. "We know that this is the same guy that killed the other two victims, and you think he sat here waiting for someone to show up so that he could kill them? That doesn't make a bit of sense. Hell, this is an isolated area; it could have been weeks before anyone other than Barnes came down this road."

"I don't think he was going to sit around and wait for someone to come down the road. I think he knew that someone would come. Whether he knew it would be Walt or not, is another matter. Keep an eye out for signs of a camp site."

Martin stopped and looked at Tate incredulously. "You're not making sense to me. How could the killer know that someone would come?"

Tate replied, "Martin, I'm betting that Walt was out here looking for a geocache. Jewel gave him a GPS just a couple days ago, and he had it with him."

Breaking in, Emma confirmed, "This is a cache site. I found it under a group of rocks not twenty feet from where Walt is now. It's also on my list. There have been four recent finds here, maybe that's how the killer knew that someone would show up. He monitors activity on the geocaching website and then picks an active site."

Tate nodded, "Let's see if we can find any sign of our UnSub."

Walking further into the dense woods, Tate scanned a clearing near the creek. He noticed a dark spot on the ground some twenty yards up and across the small stream. Crossing the water, he made his way toward what he suspected was the remains of a campfire.

Tate called out to Martin and Emma, and then pointed at the charred ground. "I'm pretty sure our UnSub camped here. As Martin joined him, Tate studied the surrounding ground and trees. "Doesn't appear that he set up any kind of shelter, no tent and probably not a tree tarp."

Perplexed, Martin looked at Tate, "How do you figure that Tate?"

Tate pointed, "No holes in the ground that would have been needed to stake a tent, no holes in the trees that would indicate a tarp. Nothing but a fire ring. He must be familiar with roughing it, because not too many people are going to camp in these woods without some sort of shelter for protection, not only from the weather, but from the wildlife."

"This area of woods backs up to the State Park," Martin reminded. "Maybe we should go over and take a look at who registered for the last week or so. Maybe our perp came in that way, and then got off the park property. Why don't you take a ride over there and check out the registrations while I go back to town? I've got to talk to Jewel before anyone else lets this leak."

"I know it's going to be a hard conversation with Jewel," Tate said, "but if you can get any questions in, try to find out if she loaded any cache sites in his GPS. I don't know if Walt has a computer, but he never struck me as the technological type. We've already got the registration logs from the Lodge, and I'll do a cross match to see if any of the campers on their log match up with anyone who came through the State Park in the last month or so."

"I'll give you a call after I've talked to Jewel, but I can tell you that Walt did have a computer. Jewel gave it to him a couple years ago at Christmas. Don't know that he ever got the hang of using it, but he did have access, if he wanted it."

Leaving the woods, Tate and Emma slid into the SUB as Martin stopped to brief the CSU team on their plans, letting them know that he expected a full report before the end of the day. At the highway crossroads, Tate and Emma turned left toward the State Park, and Martin turned right, going back to town to speak with Jewel.

When Martin reached the station, the first person he saw was Curtis Weston from the Pine Ridge Daily.

Weston stepped forward, "Martin, is it true that you team just brought Walt Mabry in? What happened to him, heart attack?"

"Weston, go back to your office and let me do my job," Martin said, and attempted to brush by the reporter. "I am not going to talk to you or anyone else until I talk with Jewel. You were friends with Walt and I'm asking you to put that friendship first and leave this alone for now. As soon as details can be released, I will make sure that you are the one I call."

Indignant, Curtis blurted, "You're right Martin, I am friends with Walt, best friends, and that's why I asked. I'd like to be there when you tell Jewel, if it's bad news. Since her Mama died, Jewel didn't have anyone but Walt and she's going to need someone with her now."

Nodding, Martin groaned, "Sorry about that Curtis, I guess I should've thought of that myself. Come on up to my office."

Entering his office, Martin motioned the other man toward a faded brown leather chair while he coordinated some necessary arrangements with his office. Martin filled Curtis in on Walt's death, and then stared at the phone wishing there was a way out of this. After a moment he sighed, "Come on Weston, we can't put this off. We'll have to take a ride out to Walt's and talk to Jewel. She's going to take it hard."

Pulling into Walt's driveway, Martin rolled the patrol car to a stop and took a deep breath. "Curtis, this is going to be rough. I talked to Jewel just last night and she was hysterical."

Jewel stepped out onto the porch of her childhood home and watched Sheriff Crawley and Curtis Weston get out of the patrol car, their hats in their hands. "Dear God, no." She took a step forward as the two men approached the porch.

"Let's go inside where we can talk, Jewel," Martin said softly.

Dry-eyed, she turned and opened the screen door, motioning them inside. "Just tell me Sheriff. I've waited so long, and I need to know."

Taking a seat in a chair across from her, Martin waited until Curtis sank down on the couch next to Jewel. "Sweetie, we found your daddy this morning." Blinking back his own tears, Martin turned his face away from her and shook his head.

Fat tears rolled from her eyes, streaming down her face to drop somewhere out of sight. Wrapping her arms around her middle, Jewel rocked, soft sobbing sounds escalating to great heaving moans. "I knew it. I did, I knew. Where...where was he? What happened?" She choked out.

Sliding closer to the young woman, Curtis slipped a supporting arm around her shoulders, and pulled Jewel tight against him.

Fingering his hat nervously in his hands, Martin murmured, "We found him out on the County Road bordering the Reservation. Jewel, I don't know any good way to say this but you need to know. Walt's death is being treated as a homicide."

Pushing away from Curtis, Jewel raised her head to stare at Martin. "You're saying someone *killed* my Daddy? I want to see him, take me to him."

Curtis spoke up, "Jules, your daddy wouldn't want you to see him that way. He'd want you to remember him the way he was. He'd want you to remember that he had a good life."

Jumping up from the couch, Jewel turned on Curtis. "Shut up, Mr. Weston! Don't you dare tell me he had a good life, not when it ended this way." Her voice broke and dropped. "It wasn't supposed to be over yet. Someone stole the years that he had left...they stole them from him and from me." Turning to face Martin, she asked, "Who did it Sheriff? Who killed my Daddy?"

Martin rubbed a hand across his face, "We don't know yet. We've got a full team investigating."

Dropping back on the couch, Jewel wept, "Oh God, this can't be happening. My Daddy didn't have an enemy in the world." Pushing tears away with the back of one hand, she asked, "Where is he? Did you take him to the funeral home?"

Martin cleared the lump from his throat. "Not yet. He's at the County Morgue, and once they're finished with the autopsy he'll be transported to the funeral home." He tried to soften the facts. "The law requires us to have an autopsy in homicide cases. Royce Wiggins, over at the morgue, promised to give you a call to let you know when your daddy's been moved to the funeral home."

As he stood to leave, Martin looked at Jewel. Her face was pale and drawn. "Jewel, I'll call you as soon as I know something on the case, but in the meantime, if you need anything you just give me or Barb a call, okay?"

The girl nodded.

Martin pulled into his driveway and went inside where Barbara waited. "Barb, it was heartbreaking having to tell Jewel about her daddy. That girl thought Walt hung the moon. I couldn't even let her see the body, ME's not through with it, and I don't really think she needs to see it anyway. It won't be like looking at the daddy she remembers. Weston stayed with her, but I told her that she can call us anytime and we'll be there for her."

Waiting until Martin wound down, Barbara finally said, "Come on, Martin, I've got dinner ready, and after you eat, you're going to out to the garage and tinker with that old car of yours. No TV, no radio, just you and your car. Then later, when you come in, you'll have this all straight in your head."

Martin rose and followed her to the kitchen, where he stooped and kissed her cheek as she sat at the table that they'd shared for the last twelve years.

CHAPTER 30

Entering the state Park, Tate drove his SUV to the faded wooden building that served as a registration office. Parking in front of the building, he turned and grabbed his cap from the backseat and pushed it down on his head. By the time he'd locked the SUV, Emma was waiting for him at the door, and together they entered the tiny wooden office. Within a few minutes, they had what they'd come for.

On the short drive back to town, Emma scanned the copied registration sheets, comparing them to the pages they'd taken from White's Lake Lodge. Nothing popped. Looking up, she caught Tate's eye and shook her head. "Nothing here. Maybe it's like you said and the perp didn't register, or maybe it's someone who doesn't have to register, like an employee."

Keeping his eyes on the road, Tate said, "I thought of that too. The park has a few paid employees that work full time. They also have a group of volunteers that help out. The lake only has paid employees, and not too many. I already have a list of everyone who works at the lake, how about you call the park and have them fax or e-mail us a list of all employees and volunteers, and we'll cross match that as well?"

Nodding, Emma pulled her cell out, and using the phone number on the letterhead of the papers, called the park and requested the names. "We should have them on e-mail by the time we get home." Silently she cursed and turned to stare out the passenger side window. *Not your home Emma, and don't start acting like it is.*

Catching her faux pas, and seeing that she was now beating herself up over it, Tate reached across the console and pulled Emma's hand from her lap, grasping it in his own much larger one. With a gentle squeeze, he felt her body relax.

The ringing of Tate's cell forced him to let go of Emma's hand. "Echo here."

"Tate, this is Daniel Westhaven. Royce asked me to call Martin and let him know that we'll have the results from Walt's post mortem ready in about four hours. I tried Martin's office and his cell, but didn't catch him, so I thought I'd give you a call. We just got Walt on the table and we've pushed everything else back. Royce has a lab tech on site and ready to pull any pharmacology or tox reports that we need stat as well."

"I appreciate that Daniel," Tate said. "You probably caught Martin out of cell range, but I'll get in touch with him. Can you deliver the reports to my house when they're completed?"

"Sure thing, that won't be a problem at all. Does Martin need a copy delivered too?"

"No, I think one will be good. When I talk to Martin, I'll have him come over and we'll review the report together. Thanks again."

Tate disconnected the call with Daniel and pushed a number on his speed dial. He listened as Martin's phone rang. A female voice came on the line, "Sheriff's phone," she answered.

Recognizing Barbara's voice, Tate said, "Barb, this is Tate Echo. I need to speak with Martin please." Tate listened as the woman talked, and then said, "Tell him to give me a call as soon as possible Barb." Disconnecting the call, Tate turned and noticed Emma's quizzical stare, "What? The man's in the shower and his overprotective wife refused to hand him the phone!"

Emma laughed for what felt like the first time in days and joked, "I'm betting that Martin's wife is a real bear when it comes to her man."

Tate grinned. "I'll take the bear any day of the week. That woman is vicious when it comes to protecting Martin."

Toggling his blinker, Tate turned into his driveway and pulled the SUV to a stop in front of the garage.

As they walked to the porch, Emma asked, "Did Martin ever say if he talked to the Babcock's? I still want to know what they took from the cache that day."

"No, he didn't say," Tate mused. "I'm guessing that with Walt being found, it slipped his mind. I really think you're off base with that theory, Em."

Pushing the front door open, Tate stepped back allowing Emma to enter, when his cell rang again. "Martin, glad you got back with me so quickly. Daniel says we should have the ME's report on Walt in a couple house, how about you stop by and we all review it together? Seven okay?"

When he entered the house, Tate was surprised to find Emma in the kitchen filling a large pot with water.

"I thought I'd make us something to eat before the report comes." Moving the pot onto a back burner of the gas stove, she bent and watched as the flame came on, and then adjusted it down before standing to meet Tate's gaze. "Now if you'll just tell me where you keep the pasta, I'll get this going while you grab a shower, if that's okay?"

After showing her where he kept the pasta and a few other essentials, Tate went to shower.

Ten minutes later, he marveled at the wonderful smells throughout the house. Making his way into the living room, he turned toward the kitchen intending to help Emma, when a knock at the front door stopped him. Thinking that it was Daniel with the report, Tate pulled the door open and was puzzled when no one was there. A cardboard box with its top folded corner over corner sat in front of the door. Looking in both directions, Tate didn't see anyone walking away. A sound from the box drew his attention and kneeling down, he unfolded the top to reveal a small yellow dog. He caught movement in the hedge lining the side of his year, and Tate raised his eyes without turning his head to see a small boy squatting in the bushes.

Reaching into the box, he gently lifted the puppy and held him in the crook of his arm. Tate pulled a folded piece of brown paper from the bottom of the box. In blue crayon, someone, probably the same someone hiding in the hedge, had written 'he was going to take him to the pound'. Dropping the paper back in the box, Tate looked at the puppy and spoke loud enough for the child in the bushes to hear.

"No pound for you. No sir. A good looking dog like you should have a home. I'll take real good care of you, fella. Of course, if the person who left you here should ever want you back, I bet we could work something out." Seeing the little boy slide further into the hedge, Tate turned to go inside before he noticed Emma standing just outside the kitchen door.

Seeing the puppy, Emma rushed forward, a smile on her face. "Where did you get that?" she asked, reaching for the tiny bundle of yellow fur.

"Not positive, but I think a neighbor kid two doors down left him. I found him in a box on the porch with a note saying he was going to the pound. Poor kid was hiding in the bushes to see if I'd take him or not."

Laughing, Emma brought the puppy's nose to within an inch of her own. "Now aren't you just about the cutest thing in the world?"

Watching Emma coo at the puppy, Tate thought what a good mother she would have been. Hugging the puppy close, Emma moved through the kitchen and into the laundry room, grabbing an empty clothes basket she pulled a clean towel from the dryer. "Let me get this little guy settled, and then we can eat. You're going to need some puppy chow pretty quick, so maybe we can run into town before Martin comes."

Tate was clearing the dishes off the table while Emma rinsed and put them in the dishwasher when they were interrupted by a knock at the door. Catching Emma's eye, Tate winked. "Hope it's not another puppy." Setting the last of the dishes on the counter, Tate moved to answer the door. "Hey Daniel, come on in."

"No time, Chief," Daniel handed Tate a thick manila envelope. "My youngest has a thing at the elementary school tonight, and I've got to get home and get cleaned up. Here's the report on Walt. You can call me or Royce if you have questions, but I probably won't be able to answer until after I leave the school."

"Sure thing. I appreciate you dropping the report off for me."

"No problem at all, it was on my way home."

Watching Daniel leave, Tate lay the folder on a tall table behind the sofa, "Hey Em, I'm going to run down to the store and grab some chow for the pup before Martin gets here. That okay with you?"

Emma appeared at the opening between the dining area and the living room, drying her hands on a kitchen towel. "Sure. That was the report?"

With a nod, Tate pointed to the unopened envelope on the table and grabbed his keys. "Fifteen minutes and I'll be back."

Emma watched Tate go and thought that they almost seemed like a normal married couple. *Don't go there Emma. You're not married to the man. You time is almost up and you know it.*

Emma went back to the kitchen and put on a pot of coffee, then picked up the pup and sat at the table to wait for Martin and Tate.

CHAPTER 31

Martin arrived first. Accepting a cup of coffee from Emma, he sat at the table across from her. Taking a sip, he announced, "Good coffee, Ms. Emma."

Hearing the front door open, Emma gently placed the puppy back in his basket and went to pour Tate a cup of coffee. Minutes later, the three officers of their respective organizations sat at the table reviewing the ME's report for Walt Mabry.

Martin spoke first. "Report says that Walt had a massive heart attack before his throat was slashed, says that all the cuts were made post-mortem. I'm damn glad he was gone before the bastard cut him."

Sipping his coffee, Tate spoke "A heart attack is the better way to go. I do wonder what started the cardiac episode. Could have been fear, or it could have been the Ketamine. We may not know for sure, but he had a pretty big dose of Ketamine in his system."

"Other than the heart attack, there's not much here that we didn't expect to see, except that Walt wasn't sexually assaulted," Emma added.

Martin shrugged, "Guess he doesn't like old men."

Shaking her head, Emma voiced her thoughts, "More likely that he didn't want to have sex with a dead man. I bet he was pissed when Walt died before he could follow his routine."

Tate looked thoughtful for a moment. "I'm guessing that he's going to go after his next victim pretty quick, since this one didn't follow the expected pattern.

Emma stood to refill their cups. "I was thinking the same thing. His signature process was thrown off balance with Walt dying before he completed his routine, and other than pissing him off, that means he didn't get the expected sense of gratification from the kill."

Martin thanked Emma with a nod and lifted his cup as she poured the dark brew into it. "So you're saying this one didn't count?"

Emma set the glass coffee pot down, "That's pretty much it, Sheriff. This UnSub follows a strict ritual with all his kills. He subdues the victim, makes his secondary cuts; arm, eye and ear, and then he rapes them before finishing with the kill cut to the throat. He's followed that exact pattern with each one, and since Walt died in the middle of his process, he's going to need another victim in order to feel gratified."

Martin whistled through his teeth, "Damn. The towns in an uproar already and when the evening paper comes out with Walt's obit, things are going to get real ugly around here. Folks are scared stiff. Down at the diner, Burt says he's not getting any business after dark with folks afraid to be out at night, and we haven't had an illegal fishing call from the lake in over a week. People are holed up at home. We've got to catch this guy and I mean now. Before anyone else gets hurt."

Tate's cell interrupted the conversation and he excused himself to take the call. Returning a few minutes later, Tate looked at Emma, "That was the county lab calling. That piece of glass that you found at the site today was confirmed as a camera lens."

Martin frowned, "You mean the bastard is taking pictures?"

Tate shook his head, "Not pictures Martin, videos. That lens was from a motion activated mini-camcorder device." Addressing Emma, he continued. "Based on the weathering on the lens you found, techs determined that it had been there no more than a day before Walt was found. Seems our guy likes to record his work."

Showing no surprise, Emma listened as Tate continued to explain how the battery powered camcorder worked to Martin. When both men were silent, Emma suggested, "You know, it's possible that the geocache owner put that camera there just to see who was finding his site, right?"Tate looked at her, "Could be, but my gut tells me that it's *his*. He's the kind of sick bastard that would like to have a souvenir of his kills."

Emma slid back into her chair, "That reminds me, were you able to talk to the Babcock's about what they might have taken from the cache that last day, Martin?"

Leaning back, Martin nodded, "I did talk to Mrs. Babcock. I just got so caught up in things when the call came in about Walt that I forgot to tell you. Mrs. Babcock said that the boys each took a present from the cache. The older boy took a deck of playing cards, and little Justin took a coin of some type."

Tate and Emma's eyes met across the table. Tate spoke first. "Did she tell you anything about the coin? Could she describe it?"

"She did. Said at first they thought it was some kind of Travel Bug, whatever that is, but then her husband looked at it and told Justin that he could take it if he left something of his in return. She claimed it was a gold-colored coin, a little bigger than a fifty cent piece and that on one side it had..."

Martin looked thoughtful for a minute. "Damn it! She said it had something that looked like the Olympic rings on one side. That's what this guy is carving into the arms of his victims." Frustration laced his voice, Martin continued, "How the hell could I have missed that? How the hell? You were right Miss Emma, it is what they take that gets them killed."

Emma patted Martin's forearm, "it's been a busy day for everyone, and sometimes it takes a quiet minute before things click. Did she say what was on the other side of the coin? When we talked to Reva she said it had words, but she couldn't remember what they were."

"No, she didn't say, but it's not too late and I'm going to call her back and see if she recalls anything else. This could be the break that we've been looking for."

Reaching for his phone, Martin scanned his call history and then pushed call. After apologizing for the disruption, Martin put the phone on speaker so that Emma and Tate could hear the conversation first hand.

Mrs. Babcock's soft voice filtered into the room, a television played somewhere in the background. "Sheriff Crawley, I really don't recall what the coin had on the other side; I just remember the three rings on one side like I told you about. Justin was real proud of it. He kept it with him all afternoon." She paused, "You know, I don't recall seeing that coin when we went back to the cabin to collect our things, and it wasn't with..." he voice broke, "It wasn't with Justin's things when we brought him home either."

A child's voice sounded in the background and Mrs. Babcock asked, "Can you hold on just a minute Sheriff?"

At the table, Martin, Tate and Emma waited, listening without hearing as she held a muffled conversation with her remaining son. Coming back on the line, Mrs. Babcock said, "Sheriff, my son says that he remembers what was on the coin. He says that there were words carved into the coin and they said 'Let the Chase Begin.' Does that mean something?"

Tate answered. "Mrs. Babcock, this is Chief Tate Echo, and while we don't know the actual significance of the coin at this time, it is something that we're following up on. Thank you very much for speaking with us, and please thank your son for helping us as well."

After Martin disconnected the call, Emma said, "That's how we're going to find this guy."

CHAPTER 32

Gavin stepped from the tiny shower in his motel room, and walked to the lone window. He parted the curtains and stared out at the parking lot. "Damn you, old man," he muttered. Reaching for the phone resting on a worn table next to the bed, he dialed the number for a local pizza place who'd printed their ad on the back of his room key. He pushed the curtains closed and pulled on a pair of faded jeans, not bothering with a shirt. Sliding his computer out of a brown leather bag, Gavin waited for the welcome screen to appear and then logged into the geocaching site. *Lots to choose from, Gav. Pick an easy one, make it fast.*

Thirty minutes later, a knock on the door pulled him away from his research.

Right on time.

Without a word, Gavin shoved a twenty into the hand of the pimple-faced teen holding his pizza.

"Thanks, mister."

Dropping the pizza box on the bed, Gavin returned to his search. Scrolling through the list of caches hidden in Shannon County, he narrowed his search to four caches, and wrote them down on a scrap of paper. "These are good ones,

Gav. Lots of finds in the last week." Clicking on the links with each site he marked two off the list. "Too close to houses or a road." His mind taunted him, *Pick one, pick one.* With his pen, Gavin drew a line through one of the two remaining sets of coordinates and pushed back from his computer.

The decision was made.

Grabbing a shirt, he slipped it on, snagged a slice of pizza from the open box, and left the motel room. His shoes clanked on the metal stairs as he jogged to the parking lot and climbed into his car.

"Here we go. It won't take long Mama, I promise you." He shoved the last bite of pizza into his mouth.

CHAPTER 33

Emma flipped her computer open and slid her chair closer to Tate so that they could both see the screen. Martin stood behind Tate and watched over his shoulder as Emma pulled up the geocaching website. Tapping her cursor into the search box, Emma typed, 'Let the Chase Begin'. Martin and Tate watched as cache sites from across the country loaded on the page.

"Man-oh-man," Martin said. "How many is that, Miss Emma?"

"Twelve so far," Emma answered. "Tate, I'm going to send this list to your e-mail so that you can print a copy. From what I've seen so far, none of these are in Shannon County but I do want to follow up on them. If I'm right, that means that there are twelve victims out there that managed to make it back to a computer and log their find before this guy got to them, but I'm betting that there are at least this many more who never made it back to log a find."

Tate glanced at Emma, then Martin. "We know that none of our vics logged the find before he showed up to claim his coin. We've got to find his next cache before anyone else does."

"I'm with you on that. So what's the plan? Martin asked.

Emma cleared her throat and smiled when both men turned to face her. "Based on everything we know about this guy, and with our working profile, it's safe to assume that right now he's frustrated and in a hurry to make another kill. Walt caused a break in his ritual and emotionally he can't accept that. He's going to strike soon. In fact, he's probably already found his next site." Her fingers clicked on the keyboard and the group watched as a list of geocaches in Shannon County populated the screen.

Stepping closer and leaning over Emma's shoulder, Martin said, "Miss Emma, there's over fifty geocaches listed there. How are we going to figure out which one he'll pick?"

"It won't be easy," Tate replied, "but we can narrow the list to those sites that fit his previous locations. We know that he's in a hurry this time, so he's not going to hit any sites that aren't active. Emma, can you narrow the search to sites that have had finds in the last week or two?"

Emma's fingers flew of the keys and they waited as the new list loaded. "Eleven sites with finds in the last two weeks."

Martin smiled. "This might work. That's a doable number if we pull in some help. We could have someone staked at each one until the bastard shows up."

Reaching over and pulling the puppy from his makeshift bed, Emma settled him on her lap before turning to Martin. "While it's true that we could have someone pull watch on each site, chances are he'd see them and back off, don't forget his penchant for video. We can't put any uniforms out there or he'll run."

Rubbing a tired hand across his chin, Martin looked from Tate to Emma. "So how do we set this guy up?" A low rumbling from her lap drew Emma's attention. Looking down she noticed that the puppy had stood, his ears perked forward. Running a hand across the animal's soft head, Emma whispered, her voice soothing the small dog. "Now, what is that all about little one?" Smiling up at Tate, she continued, "He hears something, Tate."

Just then, a knocking sounded from the other room. Laughing, Emma ruffled the dog's ears and pulled him close to her in a hug, "You did hear something, did you baby? You're going to be a fine guard dog once you grow up a little."

Tate wondered if Emma knew just how beautiful she was sitting there with that stray. Excusing himself, Tate went to answer the door. "I'm coming!" Tate pulled the door open and was surprised to see Chad Green standing on the porch.

"You got a minute, Chief?" Chad asked.

Tate stepped back and motioned the younger man inside. "Come in Chad. You looking for Martin?"

Shaking his head, Chad said, "No, Tate. I came to see you, if you've got a minute that is."

Glancing toward the kitchen, Tate said, "Sure. Come on in my office, we can speak privately there."

Leading the way down the hall, Tate stepped into his office and flipped on the overhead light. He waited for Chad to enter the room and then closed the door. Tate took a seat behind his desk, "Okay, Chad, what's so important that you'd come to my house to discuss it?"

Chad pulled his hat off and fingered it nervously before speaking. "Tate, I want you to know that I didn't have anything to do with your picture ending up in the paper, or any of the gossip that's been going on around town." Releasing a deep breath, he continued, "It's true that I wanted your job, but not that way."

Tate leaned back in his chair and stared at Chad in what he hoped was his most intimidating look. "So, do you have any idea who did start the rumors that I'm not doing my job, or that I got kicked out of the FBI?"

Chad raised his chin a notch and looked Tate in the eye, "My dad. But I wasn't sure about that until today, or I would have come to you sooner. He's my dad, and I didn't want to believe that he would do something like that, but when I confronted him, he didn't deny it."

Carefully measuring his words, Tate looked approvingly at the other man. "It took a lot of guts to tell me that Chad, and I appreciate it. Any idea what it's going to take to make it stop?"

Chad smiled and said, "I think it's all taken care of, Chief. I told my Dad that if he doesn't knock it off, that me and my wife Amy Ann will pack up and move to Nebraska. He thought that was real funny until I told him that he was going to be a grandpa in a few months, and that it would be a damn shame if his only grandson lived a whole state away."

"Chad, I won't lie to you about this. I'm far from happy that Pete would think that it's okay to ruin my reputation, but I'm not one to hold a grudge. Seems like you're holding all the cards to keep Pete in line. Of course, there will probably still be some fallout from the Sheriff once he gets a hold of Pete."

"So you're not going to pull any strings to get Dad removed from the force?"

Moving to the door, Tate hedged. "I won't, as long as he knocks it off, but you'll have to talk to the Sheriff about your dad, since he doesn't report to the city or to me. Come on in the kitchen and you can talk to him now. The Sheriff and SSA Gage-Echo are here, and we have an idea about how to catch this killer. We could use your help."

Surprise showed on Martin and Emma's faces when Tate stepped into the kitchen, followed by Chad Green. "Martin, Emma, seems we've got that help we were talking about, and congratulations are in order as well. Chad just told me that he's going to be a daddy!"

Martin extended his hand to Chad. "Now that's good news, Chad. Miss Amy feeling alright?"

Chad smiled and nodded as he took the older man's hand. "Just fine, Sheriff, but that's not what brought me by tonight. I'd like to speak privately with you for a minute, if you've got time."

With a nod toward Martin, Tate said, "Why don't you and Chad step into my office while me and Emma continue working to narrow down our search perimeters?"

Still stroking the dog in her lap, Emma waited until Martin and Chad left the room before speaking. "What's that about? Keeping the friends close and the enemies closer?"

Tate slid into the chair next to her, "Nope. Chad just confirmed that Pete is the one who started all the trouble in town, and he pulled a few cards of his own to make sure that it stops. Now what about these cache sites, where's our focus going to be?"

Emma turned to her screen and pointed. "Martin and I narrowed it down to the six most likely sites. These six are secluded enough to give the UnSub the privacy that he needs, all have had recent finds, and are relatively easy to access. I'm very confident that one of these sites will be his next kill site."

Nodding, Tate watched as Emma pulled her phone out and loaded the coordinates to all six caches into her GPS system.

CHAPTER 34

"It won't be long now." Gavin felt better than he had since that old fucker made a mess of his last hunt. He turned the car around and drove back through town toward the interstate and his grimy motel room. Spotting a flashing neon sign ahead, he pulled the car to a smooth stop in front of a convenience store. He strolled to the back of the store and pulled a six pack of beer from the cooler, and then grabbed a bag of chips from a metal rack on his way back to the counter. Laying his purchases on the counter and reaching for his wallet, Gavin stilled.

Neatly stacked newspapers sat on one side of the counter, and right there on the front page was the old man's picture. Willing his hand not to shake, Gavin pulled a paper from the stack and added it to his purchases. He slid a twenty from his wallet across the counter and waited while the cashier rang up his total, and then pushed the chips and newspaper into a plastic bag.

"You want a bag for the beer, mister?"

Shaking his head, Gavin wadded his change in his hand and pushed it into his pocket. He grabbed the beer and the plastic back, and then left the store without a word.

Back in his room, Gavin popped open a beer and leaned back on the bed. He stared at a picture of the old man he'd met just once. "Old geezer looks happier here than when I last saw him." He snorted, "He screwed you, Gav. Totally screwed you. The bastard had to go and die before you could kill him, and you didn't get it recorded either. I hope his fucking dog died, too."

Wadding the paper in his hands, Gavin threw it against the wall and watched as it bounced, and then landed near the end of the bed. He leaned back and rested one arm over his eyes. Suddenly he sat up and crawled to the end of the bed and reached to the floor where the wadded up newspaper lay. Opening the paper to the obit page, he studied the information shared in the paper. "Well, I got fucked out of watching them fin you Walt Mabry, but I can still watch them put your sorry old ass in the ground."

Feeling only slightly better, Gavin scanned the date and time or Walt's service, then pulled his grey suit from the closet, laying it neatly across the back of the only chair in the room. "Tomorrow, Walt. We meet again tomorrow." Happier than he'd been in days, Gavin swigged his beer and waited for his computer to boot up. "A little late night freak show, and you'll sleep like a baby, Gav."

A sliver of morning sun peeked through a gap in the curtains and woke Gavin the following morning. Smiling he stretched and slid out of bed to make his way to the bathroom. He turned the shower on and stepping into the hot spray he pulled the plastic curtain closed. Minutes later he stood at the bathroom sink, wiping fog from the mirror with his towel. He pulled a comb through his wet hair and said, "Got to look good today Gav, you're going to a funeral."

Three hours later, Gavin parked his red rental near the long line of cars just inside the cemetery grounds. Stepping behind a foursome of funeral goers, Gavin watched as the cemetery filled with people saying their last goodbye to Walt Mabry. A large green canvas canopy covered the grave site, and what he assumed to be family and close friends were seated on white folding chairs in the shade of the covering. Small clusters of people milled about, speaking quietly to each other. Standing near the back of the canopy, Gavin listened as a man with a bible in his hand spoke about Walt's life. Moving over a few steps he had a clear view of the rose draped coffin. Red roses. Then he stopped in his tracks.

The dog.

Seated at the head of the casket, the German Shepherd appeared to be at attention, his gaze fixed on a pretty young woman sitting on the front row of chairs. Stepping further to the side, Gavin watched the woman. Long blonde hair draped across part of her face as she stared straight ahead. Even from this distance, Gavin could see that her eyes were puffy and red, and one hand seemed to pulse around a wadded tissue. The service ended with a prayer for Jewel.

"Jewel," Gavin whispered. "What a lovely name."

Mourners came forward, forming a line that passed between the woman and the coffin. Stepping forward as their time came, people either shook her hand or gave a quick hug while whispering words that Gavin assumed were meant to comfort the young woman.

Stepping into the line, Gavin moved forward with the other mourners, head down, and a small smile on his lips. Reaching the woman, Gavin stopped. Taking her hands in his, he leaned forward and whispered, "Walt was a lot of fun... Jewel."

Her expression quizzical, Jewel looked at the man in front of her, trying to place him as a friend or acquaintance of her father, but she could do neither. A low growl pulled her attention away from the man. King had moved to sit at her side. Touching a hand to the large dog's head, she softly fussed, "Hush, King." When she looked up, the strange man had been replaced by Curtis Weston, who opened his arms and pulled her into a tight hug.

Gavin pushed through the crowd and moved toward the line of parked cars at the cemetery's edge. Reaching his car, he turned and stared back at Walt's grave, and all the people gathered there. "This is almost as good as watching them find you, Walt. I loved seeing your Jewel all torn up. Maybe she'll be the next cacher I meet."

As he reached for the door handle, Gavin noticed a Shannon County patrol car parked three spaces behind him. Sliding into the seat and adjusting the rear view mirror, he watched as an older man in uniform talked to a dark haired man with a beautiful woman at his side.

He thought he recognized the uniformed cop from the night he killed the boy. The man next to him seemed vaguely familiar too, but he couldn't really place him. He had to be ex-military, cop or both. Keeping low in the seat, he continued to watch as the woman pointed to an older couple in the crowd, smiled and said something to the man that caused him to scowl. "Wouldn't mind meeting her on a lonely road."

When the uniformed man turned to get into his patrol car, Gavin whistled, "Old cop from the cache site where I took the kid. He's just everywhere isn't he?" Turning the key, Gavin started the car, and slowly pulled away from the curb in the opposite direction of the patrol car.

Tate watched as well wishers moved, forming a line and offering their condolences to Jewel. Almost everyone in town over the age of forty had known Jewel since she was a baby, and had known Walt even longer. Tate felt a sense of pride watching his friends and neighbors come together to support one of their own.

Emma stood near the back of the line, talking quietly with his parents. A man that Tate didn't recognize stepped up to Jewel. Taking her by the hands, he leaned forward and whispered something to her. At the same time, King moved to stand at Jewel's side, her hand reached out to stroke her father's best friend on his big head. Looking up, Tate caught Emma's eye. With a short nod, she moved away from his parents, allowing them to step forward in line as she moved toward him.

Tate and Emma stood with Martin at the front of his patrol car. "See you pulled the short straw today Martin." Tate said.

Leaning back against the car, Martin replied, "Yeah, that's about the way of it. I thought it best to stop by even if I was on call. Couldn't leave the car in case something comes over the radio, since I didn't want to turn my portable on too close to the proceedings. Barb paid our respects with Jewel."

"Martin, you see that young guy with the short dark hair, he was wearing a grey suit and he walked out to the parking area just a minute ago? He got into a red rental car. I didn't recognize him, but I don't think King like him too much."

"No, Tate, I didn't see him. What makes you think that King didn't like him?"

"When the guy stepped up to Jewel, King left his post at the head of Walt's casket and moved to stand next to Jewel. I saw her say something to King and pet him. Just seemed strange to me, since King hasn't moved from Walt's casket since he got here."

Martin shrugged, "Yeah, that is a little strange. Could just be that he didn't know the guy, most everyone here is local." Walking around to the driver's side of the patrol car, he continued, "I'm going to run my patrol real quick and I'll meet you all back at the courthouse in about an hour. Chad is coming in to meet us too. I want to wrap this up and catch this bastard before he hunts again. That give you enough time?"

Tate nodded.

Emma said, "Tate, you'd better go talk to your mother a minute, otherwise, we're going to be at her house eating cake in an hour instead of tracking down a killer. I tried to beg off, but you know how stubborn she can be."

Forty five minutes later, Tate and Emma pulled into the courthouse parking lot. Martin's car was already parked in the designated spot for the Sheriff. Unlocking his office door, Tate waited for Emma, Martin and Chad to go inside before stepping in and closing the door.

"You and Miss Emma ready to do a little geocaching?" Martin asked.

Tate turned his computer on and reached into a desk drawer to pull out a small hand-held GPS and laid it on the desk in front of him. "This is Walt's GPS. I borrowed it from the evidence room. Figured if we're going to cache, then we should look like we've done it before, and serious cachers probably wouldn't use a cell phone."

Until now, Chad had stood quietly behind Martin, but seeing the GPS, he stepped forward and picked it up, turning it over in his large hand. "I've never been geocaching, can you tell me how it works before we go? I don't want to look stupid or waste time."

Walking over to where Chad stood, Emma smiled, "Sure, Chad, we'll give you a crash course and you'll be fine." Glancing at Tate, she turned to look at Martin. "Martin, I know you want this guy bad, but I don't think that you should go with us."

Martin frowned, "Why not? You know that me and Tate's been working this case together since the Parker murder, and I don't see any reason that I shouldn't be out there too."

Emma explained, "We know that the UnSub has been in the county, or in and out of the county, for the last few weeks, and he knows the area well, right?"

Martin nodded, "That's true, but what's that got to do..."

"Chances are," she said, "that he's seen you, and possibly Tate as well. We went back to Parker's house and came up empty when we searched for a camera. We know that the camera was broken at the site where Walt was found, but we don't know if he had a working camera at the Babcock scene, and you were there for a long time, right?"

Deflated, Martin sank back in his chair. "You're right. I was there from the time the boy was found until Daniel took the body to the morgue. If there was a camera there, then he probably did see me. Damn. So now what do we do? I thought we were going out in teams."

"We will go in team," Tate leaned back in his chair. "I don't want anyone out there alone."

Stepping to Tate's side, Emma said, "I agree, but what we need is a partner for Chad, or I can go with Chad and we'll find you a partner."

"You go with me, Em." Tate barked without hesitation. "How about I call Reva and see if she can help us out? She's a seasoned cacher and she's see this mystery coin before. I think she'd be willing to help us out if it means that we catch Saralyn's killer."

Tate dialed Reva's number and she answered on the second ring. Explaining the situation to her as briefly as possible, Tate said, "Thanks, Reva. Chad Green will be by to pick you up in about fifteen minutes, and he'll explain more about our plan to you then."

Agreeing that each team would take three of the six caches on their 'most likely' list Tate loaded three into Walt's GPS and highlighted the other three on Emma's cell phone. Tate and Martin watched as Emma explained to Chad how to use the GPS, and some of the general rules of geocaching.

Looking like he's just lost his best friend, martin asked, "So what can I do to help without actually going out to look for caches?"

Emma placed a reassuring hand on his arm. "We need you to be our acting command central. After each find, we'll call in and report back to you. You'll know where each team is, and if we find he coin." She turned to Chad, "If you and Reva find the coin, you are to leave it, understood? We can't have a private citizen calling our killer out. If you find it, leave the coin there and call me and Tate with the coordinates so that we can go and retrieve it."

"Last thing before we go," Tate added, "remember that you're just a hiker out for fun today. Act excited when you find the cache, laugh or something, maybe even hold hands. You know, make it look real. If the bastard is watching, we don't want to tip him off in any way."

Pushing the GPS into his jacket pocket, Chad nodded. "You can count on me, Chief. We're going to find this killer and pull the plug before anyone else gets hurt."

CHAPTER 35

Twenty minutes later, Chad drove into Miller's Haven, following the directions that Tate had given him, and found Reva's house without any problems. She was sitting on the steps when he pulled into the driveway and stood when she saw his blue truck turning in. Once Chad stopped, Reva opened the passenger side door and jumped in. Glancing over at her, Chad thought she looked tense. "You sure you're up for this?"

Reva hesitated a minute before saying, "I am definitely up to this, Chad. If I can help you guys catch Saralyn's killer, then I am with you all the way."

Grinning, Chad looked over his shoulder as he backed out of the drive. He reached into his jacket pocket and pulled the GPS out, tossing it onto the seat between them. Tate already loaded the coordinates into the GPS and I know the general area for the three caches we're responsible for."

Smiling for the first time, Reva said, "Let's do this!"

Once Tate entered White's Lake Loge Resort, Emma fed him directions until they had to park and finish the hunt on foot. Walking along the pine covered trail Tate reached out and took Emma's hand, giving it a gentle squeeze.

"Today's the day, Em. We're going to nail this bastard and put an end to this nightmare."

Smiling up at him, Emma gave his hand a reassuring squeeze. "Feels like old times doesn't it? You and me out to rid the world of one more sick killer."

Tate grinned and picked up the pace as the beeping of the GPS became more insistent. "Must be about there. Did this one have a clue?"

Emma shook her head. "Not really a clue, but the directions did say that you don't have to cross the fence, so I'm thinking that if there's a fence it must be on or near it. GPS says we need to go about fifteen feet further."

A few seconds later, the hand-held device stopped beeping and a robotic voice said, 'you have reached your destination'. Letting go of Emma's hand, Tate moved toward a barbed wire fence marking the boundary of the lodge property. "Okay, Em, move a little up and down the fence line to see if the directional arrow changes."

Taking a few steps along the fence line, Emma turned around and stopped. "Don't think I need to go any further." She pushed some leaves away from a metal fence post and reached behind it, pulling a green ammunition container from a shallow resting place under the leaves. "Not very well hidden."

Squatting next to the container, Tate slipped the clasp open and pulled the top back so that they could see inside. "Damn, it's not here." Closing the container, Tate pushed it back into the shallow indention and covered it with leaves. Glancing up at Emma, he said, "Don't look so disappointed, Em. We've still got two to go."

Tate and Emma retraced their steps to the car and got in. Turning up the air conditioner, Emma pulled her hair back and let the cool air blow in her face. "For spring in South Dakota, it sure is hot out today. So, which cache do you want to do next?"

"Load the one off County Road 17, that's the closest one to here." Pulling his cell phone from his shirt pocket, Tate handed it to Emma. "Why don't you give Martin a call and let him know to cross this one off the list."

Emma dialed Martin's number and waited while the call connected.

"Crawley here. That you Tate?"

"No Martin, it's Emma. Tate is driving. You can cross the first Whites Lake cache off our list. No coin there. Have you heard from Chad and Reva yet?"

"Just got off the phone with Chad. They didn't have any luck with their first one either. They're on the way to their second cache site, too. I sure hope one of you finds it soon, and we don't have to widen the search to pull in more cache sites."

"Don't worry Martin, we'll find the coin and I'm certain that it's going to be at one of the six sites we've targeted. If not, then we just have to open the search up further, and maybe even pull in more help if we run short on time. I fully intend to have that coin in my hand before the day's end."

Disconnecting the call, Emma turned to Tate, "Chad and Reva came up empty handed with their first pick too."

Tate frowned, "I heard what you told Martin and I appreciate all that you've done to help us with this case, especially since you're working off the grid and could possibly lose your job if this gets out, but there is no way in hell that you're walking away from a cache site with that damned coin in your hand I won't let you make a target of yourself that way."

Opening her mouth to argue, Emma stopped when Tate raised his hand. "I know what you're going to say and you can just save it. Nobody but me walks away with that coin. Nobody."

Staring at him, Emma watched his hands tighten on the steering wheel, his knuckles turning white. His posture pretty much said it all. The muscle ticking on his jaw, the eyes straight ahead. Oh yeah, she'd seen that look before. With a sigh she turned and stared out the passenger side window. Some things just don't change, no matter how much you want them to, she thought. Anger bubbled up from somewhere deep within her; from the place she'd buried it when they'd divorced. Well, she wasn't married to him now, and she didn't have to hold her feelings inside any more. "Tate, pull over."

Tate recognized the look. *Oh shit, here it comes.* He thought. Steering the car to the side of the road, he eased to a stop and pushed the gearshift into park. *Might as well get it over with*, he thought, and turned to face her without saying a word.

"Tate Echo, I have never met a more stubborn man in my entire life! Comments like that last one make me want to pull my service revolver and just shoot some sense into you, or put you out of your misery, whichever comes first! I am a trained agent for the damned Federal Bureau of Investigation, and I am perfectly capable of handling myself without any advice or protection from you. In case you don't remember, comments just like that one, caused our divor..."

Before she could say another word, Tate hauled her against his chest and covered her mouth with his own in a punishing kiss, his tongue exploring her mouth in a violent dance that commanded her senses. Breaking the kiss, Tate leaned back against the seat and struggled to get his breath under control.

Staring at Emma's flushed and confused face, he said, "And that, Emma, is a big part of why we got married in the first place."

Starting the car, Tate punched the gas pedal. He jerked the wheel, moving the SUV back onto the road. Behind them, a spray of loose gravel peppered the dirt.

Staring straight ahead, Emma fought to regain her composure and her own breath. Damn, that man could kiss, now if she could just yank out his vocal cords, he'd be perfect! The GPS broke their silence, instructing them to turn right at the next intersection.

Grabbing her phone from the console, Emma stared at the GPS app on the device. "Two miles further, then we have to walk."

Passing a large, white, frame farmhouse with dark green shutters, Tate pointed, "That's Walt Mabry's house. I expect that Jewel will eventually put it on the market, she has a house just outside of town herself."

Turning in her seat and catching a glance of the house as they passed, Emma whispered, "Maybe not. That's all she has left of her dad now."

"How much further?" Tate asked.

"Just over a mile"

Instructing Tate to pull over, Emma watched as he maneuvered the SUV as far off the road as he could. "Try to look happy, Em. We're supposed to be having fun here. Chances are, he's watching." Taking her hand, Tate looked at the GPS then pulled Emma along as he cut through the high weeds on the roadside. Following the directions, they walked side-by-side, still holding hands.

Pulling on Tate's arm, Emma held the GPS up to him. "We need to cut to the right here."

Tate stepped over a fallen tree and looked around at the landmarks, then at the sun hanging high in the mid-day sky. "We're almost back to Walt's property line. Surely it's not hidden on his land."

Stopping, Emma turned to him. "It's going to be here, I just know it. This human time bomb thought it would be funny to hide his cache on the property of his last victim."

Stepping up the pace, Emma took the lead as they walked single file through the wooded area. The dense trees offered a respite from the sun's hot rays, but the native white rock littering the ground slowed their progress. Stopping, Emma consulted the GPS and whispered to Tate. "No more police talk, Chief. We're just two cachers out for fun from here on out. The cache is about a hundred feet straight ahead."

Tate pointed, "The fence running here is Walt's fence. I can actually see the top of his shop building from here."

Turning to look in the direction Tate pointed, Emma nodded. "Here we go, Tate. This is it."

Forty feet later, Tate pulled Emma close and planted a quick kiss on her lips. A little more loudly than necessary, he said, "Bet I find it before you do!"

With a grin, Emma asked, "So what do I get if I find it first?"

Swatting her on the butt and snatching the GPS from her hand, Tate laughed, "No need to set the stakes, because this cache is all mine, babe."

Separating, Tate and Emma scanned the area looking for the hidden cache.

"I found it!" Emma shouted.

Pulling a small round metal container from under a pile of rocks stacked against a fallen tree, Emma held it up as Tate walked to where she was kneeling.

Dropping down, he said, "Open it up, Em, let's see what's in it."

Pulling the top off the container, Emma removed a small wire bound tablet first, and setting it aside, she peered into the container. She reached to the bottom of the container and pulled out the coin. Knowing that they could be on camera, she held the coin skyward between her thumb and forefinger before speaking, "Check this out. Think it's some kind of Travel Bug or Cache Coin?"

Tate wanted to scream. *I told her not to touch that damn coin.* Reaching to take the token from Emma, he was surprised when she jerked away from him and jammed the coin into her front jeans pocket. She laughed, "You're not taking my treasure! I found it fair and square and I'm the winner, so now tell me what my reward is."

Knowing how angry Tate was with her, Emma moved close to him and wrapped her arms around his neck. Standing on tip toes, she pushed her lips against his and quietly murmured, "Don't blow this Tate. It may be our only shot."

Growling under his breath, Tate pulled her closer, covering her mouth with his in a toe curling kiss that turned hungry in an instant.

Emma swore. This was getting to be a real habit with the two of them, but right now she didn't care. Maybe he was punishing her for taking the coin. No, if that were the case, the he'd be punishing them both. Pulling her lips from his and hugging him tightly, her mouth pressed against his ear and she whispered, "You trying to give our killer a jumpstart or what?"

Breaking away, Tate locked eyes with Emma. "That, sweet Em, was the beginning of your reward for finding the cache before me. Now put the container back and let's get home so that I can finish *rewarding* you."

Laughing for the camera, Emma turned and snapped

the lid back on the container and pushed it against the tree and covered it with rocks and leaves. She stood and took the hand that Tate offered. Without talking they walked away from the cache site.

A quarter mile away, Gavin watched his computer monitor as the couple on the screen found the cache, and took his coin. When the man pulled the woman into a tight hug and let his hand drift low on her ass, Gavin whistled. "This one is going to be a lot of fun, just look at that fine little ass." Gavin moved closer to the screen, squinted, and then pushed a button to zoom in the screen in on their faces. "Shit! It's the same couple that was talking to that old Sheriff at Walt's funeral this morning!" Letting the screen slide back to full, he reasoned, *It's a fucking set-up, Gav. They think they're going to catch you!* Gavin laughed at the absurd idea, "They think they're going to catch *you!*"

Staring at the retreating backs of Tate and Emma, he snarled, "Let the chase begin, assholes. This is one game you just can't win." Watching as his tracking program loaded onto the screen, Gavin stood and walked into the kitchen, pulling a carton of orange juice from Walt Mabry's refrigerator. With the glass in hand, he moved back to the den and peered through the blinds just in time to see Tate and Emma drive past on their way back to town. Silently he held the glass up, a toast to his next victim.

CHAPTER 36

Back in the SUV, Tate pulled his cell out and punched in Martin's number. Martin answered on the first ring. Skipping the hellos, Tate said, "We've got it. Call Chad and Reva off the search, and ask them to stop by my place before Chad takes Reva home. I want her to see the coin and confirm that it's the same one she and Parker found."

"Son of a bitch, Tate. That's good news. I'll get them on the phone now, and then I'll meet you at your house."

"I don't think that's a good idea. This guy is probably already tracking us and I don't want him to see you, and for damn sure no cop cars at my place. In fact, I'm calling Julie and having her cancel all patrols in my neighborhood for now. We want to keep it as low key and quiet as possible around my place for now."

"You're right about him recognizing me, but I think we should have a couple guys out that way in plain clothes. No sense in putting you and Emma at any greater risk than necessary. I'll call Chad and get back with you on it."

Once he'd disconnected the call with Martin, Tate turned his anger on Emma, "You just had to take the damned thing, didn't you Em? You should have let me have it, but no, you had to hold it up and make sure that he saw you with it. Why? Why do you have to be the hero here?"

Pulling one leg up in the seat, Emma stared at Tate. "Just table it for now, Tate. What difference does it make which one of us got it? For God's sake, we're going to the same house. And for the record, there are no heroes here. We both have a job to do and that's what we're doing. No contest, no heroes, just a job."

Emma watched as Tate opened his mouth to speak and then clamped it shut without saying a word. With a sigh, she turned away from him. *Damn, he knows I'm right for once,* she thought.

Pulling the SUV into the driveway, Tate got out, slammed the door behind him, and walked to the porch without waiting for Emma. "You don't have time to fight with her now," he muttered under his breath.

Before he got the back door open, a tan Dodge truck pulled into the drive and Chad and Reva stepped out. Meeting Emma halfway across the yard, the three of them walked to the porch together. Pushing the door open, Tate let them all inside where they followed him to the kitchen.

Emma went to the laundry room, opened the door and scooped the puppy up in her arms, his wet pink tongue lapped out at her face as she crooned to him. She let him out for a minute then returned to the kitchen. She took a seat at the table next to Tate.

Tate spoke first, his eyes on Em the whole time, "Show Reva the coin."

Emma reached into her jeans pocket and pulled the token out, laying it on the table in front of Reva.

Without touching it, Reva nodded. "That's it. That's the same coin that me and Saralyn found at the lake." Overcome with emotion, Reva buried her face in her hands before looking up and Tate, and then at Emma. "Oh, my God, he's going to come after you now. I know that's what you wanted but...well...I guess it wasn't so real until now."

Emma moved to the chair next to Reva, placing a comforting arm around the other woman's shoulders. "It's okay, Reva. It's different this time. Tate and I know that he's coming, we'll be ready and we'll catch him. You don't have to worry about us."

Reva wiped at the tears forming in her eyes. "I know, Emma, but I keep thinking about Saralyn and how that could have been me. I don't want anything to happen to you or Tate, either." With a strangled sigh, she whispered, "I'm afraid for you both."

"You don't have to be afraid," Chad said. "Tate and Emma are both trained to handle situations like this and they're going to be fine. Come on, let me take you home."

With a nod, Reva stood and gave Emma a quick hug. She turned to Tate. "Tate you take real good care of the two of you. I don't have too many friends, and I can't bear to think of losing another one."

Tate gave Reva a peck on the cheek. "I won't let you down." Turning to Chad, he said, "Can I speak to you for a just a minute before you leave please?"

Tate opened the back door and the two men stepped out onto the deck, leaving the women in the kitchen. He needed some extra protection now that Em's life was on the line.

CHAPTER 37

Just a few more hours, Gav and you'll have your coin back and a little fun too. Then my friend, it's time for you to get the hell out of Pine Ridge for good. Grabbing his backpack and pushing his computer inside, he walked to the back door of Walt's house. It had been the perfect hiding place, completely deserted since Walt's death. Gavin took the steps two at a time, making his way to the old barn in the back, where he'd parked his car out of sight. *Wouldn't want the lovely Jewel coming by and finding you in her daddy's house, now would you?*

Dropping his backpack on a weathered work table in the barn, Gavin reviewed the items that he would need. *Could need two needles, Gav. Chances are, wherever the hot chick went, the guy went too.* He pulled a pocket knife from his front jeans pocket, and then measured and cut four lengths of red cording from a spool stored in his backpack. Staring at the cording, he pulled two more lengths and cut them. *Better to be over prepared than under, and that's one big dude.*

Repacking his backpack, Gavin tossed it into the front seat of his car, and then sat down in the driver's seat without starting the vehicle. Laying his head back against the seat, he closed his eyes and willed his body to relax.

I told you it wouldn't take long, Mama. Just think, after tonight, there will be five more people just like you, and these five are really special, Mama. They all live right here in Pine Ridge. That old man, Walt, probably lived here when you did. He probably looked the other way when you'd come to town all busted up, just like the others did. Now they know what it's like. Now they're all just like you, Mama...Just like you.

CHAPTER 38

Emma sat in the living room floor, playing tug of war with the puppy using an old sock. She watched Tate from the corner of her eye. "Why don't you sit down? You know as well as I do that he's not coming until dark. This is a well-populated area and he wouldn't risk it. Save that energy for later, could be that you'll need it then."

Frowning at her, Tate flopped down on the couch and propped his feet on the smooth wooden surface of the coffee table. Grabbing the remote from the arm of the sofa, he flicked the television on and started surfing the channels.

The third time that Tate passed the same channel, Emma stood, bringing the puppy with her. Taking a seat next to him, she bumped her shoulder against his, "Talk to me."

He grunted, "And exactly what good would that do me, Emma? I don't think you listen to me."

Emma drew in a deep breath, "Tate, you're not being fair. I listen to you when you talk. It's when you try to pull some non-existent rank, and give me orders that we run into issues. I don't want to argue, I just want to talk."

Leaning forward, Tate rubbed his face with his hands before speaking. "You're right. I know you're right, but I can't help myself. I want you to be safe. If you had listened and let me take the coin, you could be at the courthouse with Martin, safe and sound right now, instead of sitting here waiting for a killer."

She shook her head, "I don't think you'll ever understand. I don't want to sit at the courthouse, safe and sound with Martin or anyone else. A desk job would drive me crazy. I like what I do."

Seeing that he was about to speak, Emma cupped a hand on his cheek, silencing him, "It makes me feel good knowing that I'm helping the world be a better place when I take down a killer, a molester, a drug runner or any other criminal out there. I couldn't get that from a desk job. You of all people know about the satisfaction that comes from being part of a field team."

Looking into her eyes, Tate felt helpless. The anger drained from his body, deflating him like a left-over party balloon. "I know, Em...I know."

Opening her arms and pulling him into a hug, Emma sprayed tiny kisses on his neck. Tate buried his face in her hair, inhaling the freshness and the unique scent that was all Emma. God he wished they could sit like this forever. A tiny yelp broke them apart. Looking down, Emma pulled the puppy from the sofa between them, his little tail slashed back and forth as he tried to lick her.

With a playful growl, Tate rolled the puppy on his back, scratched his tummy for a minute, and then carefully sat him on the floor. "You know he thinks you're his mama, right?"

Emma turned to Tate and smiled, "I know, and maybe he's right. I'm pretty fond of the little guy. You're going to keep him, aren't you Tate?"

"Don't suppose you'd consider staying here and helping take care of him? Wait, don't answer that. I already know the answer, and I don't want to hear it out loud. Not yet."

Scooting closer, Emma laid her head on Tate's chest, one hand resting on his muscular thigh. "It's almost dark. He's coming soon."

Tate ran his fingers through her long hair, and leaned one cheek against her head. They sat like that for more than ten minutes before he finally said, "I guess we'd better get ready. We want the bastard to feel welcome when he shows up." Tate stood and walked to the living room windows and twisted the rod to open the blinds. "Turn the lamp cn, Em. We want him to be able to see us if he comes from the front."

Emma pulled her shoes on, switched on the lamp, and then picked the puppy up. "I'm going to take the pup for a potty run before it gets crazy around here."

"Okay, but don't leave the deck, and take your gun. It's not really dark enough for him to be slinking around yet, but don't chance it. I'm going to check the windows in the other rooms. When the bastard shows up, I want to limit his way in to the doors only."

CHAPTER 39

Hunching in the bushes on the edge of the yard, Gavin adjusted his backpack and sat down. Did they really think he was too stupid to reccgnize a trap when it practically crawled up his leg and bit him on the ass? Next to him on the ground lay the unconscious body of the cop they'd posted to keep him out.

Kicking the man with one foot, Gavin muttered, "Good thing I brought extra cord. Once the K wears off, you're going to have a hell of a headache, man."

Light filtering out from the back door of the house pulled Gavin's attention away from the downed cop. The woman that took his coin appeared on the deck with a small puppy. "Damn, they really do think that I can't get to them." Stepping back into the hedge, Gavin pushed his way through the dense shrub, and popped out in the yard next door. With his back to the bush, he ran a few feet down the hedge row before pushing back through and jogging a short distance to the side of the house. Using the shadows for cover, Gavin peeked around the corner of the house and watched the woman as she sat the dog down on the ground where he promptly began sniffing the grass.

Crouching low, Gavin dropped to his knees. Hugging the shadows at the side of the house, he crawled, stopping only when the house met the deck. He practically smelled the bitch from here.

Just a few more feet. He thought and fought to control the excitement bubbling inside him.

A voice from inside the house boomed and Gavin froze.

"Em, what's the holdup out there?"

Turning toward the house, the woman yelled into the door, "Just about finished. He has to find the right spot!"

Night was falling fast now, the yard was almost black. Fireflies flashed their blinking tails. Calling the puppy, the woman sighed with frustration when he just looked up at here and then turned away to chase a bug in the grass. She stepped off the deck and moved quickly toward the pup. "Time to go in little guy, it's too dark to be chasing bugs." Bending over, she scooped the puppy up in her arms.

That's when Gavin saw it. The gun wedged at the small of her back. The black metal reflected in the glow from the porch light.

Stupid bitch. Come to me. Just a few more steps and you're mine. He thought.

Emma never saw the man coming. Lunging from the shadows, he knocked her down. Landing on her back, his body covered hers as he clamped a hand across her mouth. The fall knocked the air from her lungs and catching a breath seemed impossible. Struggling, she tried to free herself. The puppy yipped and fell from her hands to land somewhere in the darkness.

Emma felt his hand slide around to her back and pull her gun free from where it was tucked inside her pants.

Leaning close, he whispered, "I'm going to pull you up now, and we're going to take a little walk. If you make even one sound, I will shoot you. Got it?"

Emma nodded and allowed him to pull her to her feet, the gun stayed pointed at her chest.

"Hold your hands out," he hissed, pulling a piece of red cording from his pocket. Gavin quickly tied her hands, keeping one eye on the back door to the house. He pushed the woman in front of him as they slithered around the corner of the house and ducked back through the hedge, making their way behind the house next door and out into the alley where his car was parked.

Her breath regained, Emma thought, *You cannot get in that car. Think. If you scream, he's going to shoot you, and if you go with him, that will be even worse. You've to stall and give Tate time to find you.* Balking at the door of the car, Emma turned and kicked at her captor, striking him on the thigh. *Damn, missed.*

"You crazy bitch!" Gavin raised the gun and slammed it against her head. The last thing Emma heard before passing into oblivion was Tate's voice calling to her.

"Emma! Emma, where are you? Damn it, I should have known you wouldn't stay on the deck." The puppy ran up to Tate and sniffed his boot. *Where was she?* The slamming of a car door and an engine firing pushed Tate into a full-out run. Pulling his gun as he ran toward the sound, Tate stepped into the alley just as a car spun out, spraying him with gravel. Raising his revolver, Tate shot at the tires, but the car didn't slow.

"Shit!"

Running for his SUV, Tate pulled his cell out and hit the last number called, "Martin, the bastard's got Emma."

"Whoa there Tate, slow down."

"No time, Martin. He was parked in the alley that runs behind my house. A compact car, couldn't get the make or model, but it's a dark colored sedan. Maybe red."

"What about Chad? I thought he was stationed in the backyard." Martin questioned.

"No sign of Chad when I came outside, so send someone over to search. This guy could have both of them, for all I know. The alley would have forced him to the right on Magnolia Street but where he's headed after that, I don't know. I've got to go." Tate turned right from his driveway and punched the gas pedal to the floor.

He paused at the end of the street trying to decide which way to go. Deciding that the killer wouldn't want to drive through the middle of town now that he knew he'd been spotted, Tate turned left. A mile down the road he slowed when tail lights appeared in the distance.

Just hang back, Tate, be patient, and let him show you where he's going.

Gavin glanced at Emma slumped in the front seat. Reaching over, he placed two fingers on her neck, feeling for a pulse. *The bitch is alive. For now anyway.* Glancing in the rearview mirror, Gavin spotted headlights about a quarter mile back.

"Shit. Just play it cool, Gav. They're not gaining on you." A mile down the road, Gavin took a right turn without breaking; dust billowed up behind the car as the rear end fishtailed. *Almost there Gav, almost there.* He thought.

Emma groaned, the movement of the car careening around a turn caused bile to boil in the back of her throat. Without moving her body, she opened one eye a sliver and stared at the killer. She tried to see beyond him to determine where they were going. No luck.

Just stay still Emma. Make him have to carry you out, and just maybe you can get the upper hand.

Tate watched as the car ahead turned without hitting the brakes, and saw the tail lights pull a fast back and forth pattern. "Damn, he's going to Walt's place, or back to the cache site where we found the coin...if he doesn't wreck before he gets there."

Without slowing, Tate drove past the road that the killer turned on, planning to double back once the coast was clear. Pulling his phone out, Tate called Martin. "He's either going back to the cache site, or he's going to Walt Mabry's place, there's nothing else on that road. I let him go without following, but I'm turning around now. I didn't want to spook him, not with Emma in that car."

"I'm on my way. I'll get some back up out that way too."

"No, Martin, don't come in with lights and sirens blazing. I don't want to scare him or have him get in a hurry. I'm going to park and walk, hopefully taking him by surprise. The last thing we need is for someone to come up like the damned Calvary. If you get here in time, walk in and keep it quiet. Sound carries a long way out here."

"I've got you're back on this one. You be careful out there, and bring our Miss Emma home safe."

Martin glanced at his wife standing in the doorway with his gun and hat in her hands. "You know me so well, sweetheart. I'll be back as quick as I can." Kissing her on the lips, Martin slipped his hat on and pulled his gun belt around his waist. He hoped that he hadn't just lied to his wife, and that they would all be back safe and out of harm's way soon.

CHAPTER 40

Gavin jumped from his car and ran toward the barn. He grabbed one of the large wooden doors and pulled it open wide enough to drive through. He killed the engine and stepped out to close the barn door, glancing at Emma still slumped in the front seat. *Must have hit the bitch pretty hard.*

As soon as Emma heard the car door close, and his footsteps moving away, she frantically twisted her wrists, trying to free her hands before he returned. *Damn it,* she thought. *They're too tight.* She heard his footsteps again and let her body slump back in the seat.

Tate let his vehicle coast slowly down the dirt road, even though it was now too dark for anyone to see any dust being raised. A half mile from Walt's house, he pulled over, the wheels dipped into the ditch and gravel and rocks crunched under the tires as he braked. Pulling a flashlight from the glove compartment, he turned it on as he slid from the SUV, but kept the beam low to the ground. He eased the door closed with his hip, the loud metallic click echoed into the still night and Tate winced.

Following the road, Tate jogged to Walt's driveway and slipped into the foliage on the fence line, making his way closer to the house. *No lights. Shit, maybe they're not here.* A creaking sound from behind the house caught Tate's attention.

The barn.

Taking a chance, Tate ran from the cover of trees to the side of Walt's house. He kept to the shadows and walked to the rear corner of the house. Here he had a clear view of the barn. Both the main doors were closed, but a faint glow of light peeked eerily from a two inch crack at the bottom. He took a deep breath. *Now what?*

Gavin pulled the passenger door open and shook Emma's arm. "Time to wake up, bitch. The chase is over, but the party is just beginning, and I want you awake for it." He shook her hard and waited a few seconds for her to respond. "Shit. She's out cold." Reaching inside the car, Gavin locked one arm around Emma's waist and hoisted her out before dropping her on the barn floor.

Emma resisted the urge to tense when he touched her. *You probably won't get another chance at this.* She thought. Her butt hit the hard-packed dirt floor of the barn with a thud. Letting her body roll back, Emma brought her feet up, kicking at the man with all her strength.

A solid blow to the mid-section knocked Gavin off his feet. He fell back on the floor of the barn and was surprised for a minute, and then he laughed. The woman struggled to stand and failed so she tried scooting backward toward the door. Gavin pulled a length of red cord from his pocket and advanced on her. "You're going to be so much fun. I love it when they fight."

As soon as the man was close enough she kicked at him again, her blow glanced off his thigh. This time he was ready for her, and when she kicked, he grabbed her ankle and twisted, forcing her face down on the floor. He wrapped the cord around her ankles and pulled it tight, and then stepped back. "Now, where's my coin bitch?"

Emma rolled over and looked at the crazed man in front of her, knowing that if she gave him the token that he would have no reason to keep her alive. "Why is the coin so important to you? It's nothing but a toy, it doesn't have any value." She asked.

Watching his face twist with anger, Emma knew that she'd hit a nerve. The killer loved that damn coin. *Just keep him talking Emma.*

Kicking her on the leg, Gavin pointed to the computer sitting on a wooden work table behind him. "I know that you have it, in fact, I always know where it is, so give it to me."

Scooting back further from his reach, Emma faltered. "Okay, so I have it. Why don't you tell me about the coin? What's so special about it, and why do you put it in geocaches and then kill the people who find it?"

Slamming his hand down on the hood of the car, Gavin snapped. "Enough!" Turning, he walked to the work table and opened his backpack, and pulled a syringe out. He twisted the orange safety cap off. Holding the needle up to the soft light of the computer screen, he pushed the clear liquid upward until a drop oozed from the needle. He gave it a good thump.

"Maybe you'll be a little more helpful once you fall into the K-hole, bitch. Actually, you won't be helpful at all, but then you won't care if I do a little body search either."

Trying to scoot further away, Emma realized that she'd moved as far as she could, her back now rested against the barn door. "No need for that, I'll give you the coin."

Rushing her, Gavin jabbed the needle into her upper thigh, pushing the drug into her muscle. "You, you will give me my coin, or I'll just take it after I'm through with you, doesn't matter much to me at this point."

Emma stared at the man in front of her. His mouth moved but she couldn't hear his words over the loud buzzing in her ears. "What..." She tried to speak but gave up, leaning her head back on something hard. The barn walls pulsed in and out like a strange house of mirrors and panic filled her gut as she stared at the man standing over her. *This is it.* She struggled, but failed to move.

Smiling, Gavin watched the woman, knowing the exact instant that she fell into the K hole. "You're there now. Pretty cool, huh?" He walked to the work bench and pulled a small gray plastic case from his backpack. He flipped the case open and ran his finger across a set of small blades. He smiled, "It's time now, Mama. But first, I get to have a little fun." Taking the knives with him, Gavin knelt next to Emma.

Outside, Tate slid closer to the barn. *It's too quiet in there. There's got to be another way in, it's too big to only have one door.*

Tate heard Emma asking the killer about his coin and why it was important to him. *That's it Em, just keep him talking.*

Sliding around to the side of the barn, Tate let his hands glide against the rough wood, feeling for a door or loose board. He turned the corner and walked along the rear of the barn. He had gone only a couple of feet when he felt it. A door. Gripping the iron door knob, he slowly turned it. The door opened without a sound. Sliding into the dark room, Tate squinted, letting his eyes adjust before seeing a faint glow of light coming from the wall in front of him.

Thank God. He heard them clearly now. Was the killer talking to his mother? Was there someone else in there too? Tate counted to three before he pushed the door open.

"Police! You touch her with that knife and you're a dead man."

Tate took in the scene before him in a flash. Emma in a near-comatose state, her back propped against the barn door, her head tilted at an unnatural angle, the killer squatting next to her with a knife in one hand and Emma's arm in the other.

"Drop the knife and stand up. Do it! Move away from her." Tate demanded.

Looking back at the woman, Gavin shrugged his shoulders, and rising to his full height he turned, lunging at the man with the gun, the knife raised above his head.

"Get down!" A voice boomed from the doorway, startling both men.

Tate fell, pressing his body to the floor, his gun still drawn, eyes locked on the killer. He couldn't take the shot, he wouldn't risk hitting Emma.

Gavin saw the old sheriff standing in the doorway for a split second before the shot rang out, echoing into the night.

The old bastard shot me! Gavin dropped to the hard barn floor, the knife flew from his hand. Struggling to stand, he cried and fell back, his voice gurgled as blood seeped into his mouth. "Mama, I've got to get to Mama. She needs me."

Martin kneeled at the dying man's side. "Just lay still, we'll get an ambulance on the way, but I don't think you'll be seeing your mama anytime soon."

Looking at the killer's chest, Martin sighed. It was a clean shot, an accurate shot...a killing shot. "What's your name?" he asked.

His eyes wide with fear, Gavin coughed blood from his mouth. Looking at the sheriff he saw the ugly truth in his eyes, it was over, he was done. With his last breath, Gavin looked at the uniformed man and said, "Fuck you."

Tate jumped up and ran to Emma. He pulled her face

around to his and felt for a pulse, even though her eyes were clearly open. "Damn it. It's way too fast." Juggling his cell with nervous hands, he dialed 911 and demanded an ambulance be sent to Walt's house. "Come to the back, near the barn, and hurry!" He scooped Emma into his arms, and rushed out of the barn and into the cool yard, hoping that the fresh air would help bring her around.

How much did he give her? Tate worried. The stuff had killed Walt almost immediately and Emma was a lot smaller. "Where the hell is that ambulance?" Dropping down on one knee, he let Emma's body slide down to the cool grass. "Hold on, Em. I hear the sirens; they're almost here, baby."

Standing over the killer, Martin shook his head. Damn, he hated killing, even when killing was the right thing to do. He double checked that the man was actually dead and was relieved that there was no pulse at all. Martin left to check on Tate and Emma.

"Miss Emma going to be alright?" he asked, kneeling down next to them.

"I think so, she starting to come around, but her heard is pounding. What about our serial?" Tate asked, looking up at his friend.

"Dead. I see the ambulance lights. Won't be but a minute now."

The paramedics pulled to a smooth stop a few feet in front of Tate and Emma, and two county cruisers pulled in behind it. A squat and balding man in a blue uniform rushed to Emma's side, plugged his stethoscope into his ears and bent to listen to her heart.

"Ma'am, can you tell me your name?" No response. Pulling her right eyelid open wide, he flashed a pen light across her face.

"She was injected with Ketamine," Tate said. "I don't know how much, but it happened sometime in the last hour and a half."

Rounding the ambulance, a tall thin woman pushed a gurney through the damp grass, and stopped behind her partner.

The short man barked orders to his partner, "Pupils are responsive, BP is one sixty over ninety-eight, pulse one forty. Respiration is shallow, but steady. We're going to need a twelve lead and an IV for the ride, Susan." He turned to Tate. "We're taking her to County for some observation, Chief Echo. Ketamine generally wears off in a couple hours or so, and I expect she'll come around by the time we get her to the hospital and they get her stabilized."

Placing a hand on Tate's shoulder, Martin insisted, "You go on with her, Tate." He gestured to the two county deputies behind him. "Me and the boys have got the scene covered. We'll wait for the coroner and CSU team. You can come by my office and give your statement tomorrow."

Nodding, Tate watched the paramedics' load Emma onto the gurney, his heart was still beating out of his chest. What if he hadn't found her in time? What if Martin hadn't shot the guy when he did? What if Emma had overdosed from the Ketamine? What if? It was all that Tate could think about.

CHAPTER 41: Three Days Later

The bell over the diner door clanked when Tate and Emma walked in. Martin was drinking coffee in a booth near the door. Standing until Emma was seated, Martin said, "Miss Emma, it is real good to see you up and around." Emma laughed, "It's good to be up and around Martin. I can't thank you enough for coming to my rescue. Tate told me what you did, and I owe you one."

Grinning at Emma and then Martin, Tate said, "We both owe you one hell, the whole town owes you one."

His face turning a dark shade of red, Martin cleared his throat. "Did you find out anything on Gavin Wheeler when you called the Little Rock police?"

Tate shook his head. "Some. He was raised there, a good student but a loner, no trouble with the law. His mother lives in a very upscale Alzheimer's clinic that he paid for, and will continue to pay for, through a trust that he'd set up to cover her expenses well beyond her life expectancy. Seems he actually loved his mom."

Martin nodded, "It's good news too that Chad Green will be okay. Just a crack on the head, but he's good to go, I think."

"Yes," Tate agreed, "It could have been way worse for everyone involved."

"The bureau has closed three cold cases fitting the same profile as the Pine Ridge cases, and they're looking at several more," Emma said, changing the subject. "I caught a little hell for being involved without prior approval, but since the case got solved, it's not going to be a problem."

"That's great, Miss Emma," Martin said. "Anytime they don't want you over at the FBI, you've got a spot on my team."

"Aww...That's sweet. Unfortunately, duty calls. I've got a flight out tomorrow, but I'm sure going to miss you."

Martin shook Tate's hand. "I've got rounds and county patrol today, but I'll be seeing you at the courthouse." He was surprised when Emma stood and pulled him into a fierce hug.

"Sheriff Crawley, you are one special man." Emma said, pulling back to drop a kiss on Martin's cheek.

Watching Martin leave the diner, Tate pulled a laminated menu from behind a chrome napkin dispenser, and slid his chair closer to Emma. "It's out last night together, Em, want to make it memorable and have the meatloaf special?"

"Absolutely," Emma grinned as Reva stepped up to take their order.

CHAPTER 42

Tate pulled the SUV into a parking spot at the Pine Ridge Airport and turned to Emma. "You could stay, you know that."

Cupping his face with her hand, she said, "You could come with me."

Last night had been a long awaited dream and Tate didn't want it to end. He pressed her palm against his lips, squeezing her hand gently. "Thank you for coming to my rescue."

Bright tears filled Emma's eyes and she nodded, afraid to speak and still arguing with herself. *Damn it Emma, why don't you just stay? You love him, you know you do. He loves you too. No! Stop it! You know you can't stay, you always knew you couldn't stay, nothing's changed. Suck it up, buttercup, and get on that plane.*

Silently they walked together into the Pine Ridge Airport, Tate pulling Emma's baggage behind them.

Tate's heart ached, but he would not beg her to stay. It was her call, and he'd known all along that she would leave. At least she was leaving in one piece, and if nothing else he was grateful for that. Reaching the security gate, Tate pulled Emma against him, his lips gently touching hers.

Emma wrapped her arms around his neck, pulling him closer as her fingers sneaked into the base of his hair. Emma gave him one last squeeze, took a deep breath and then turned and stepped through the security controlled gate without looking back.

"I love you, Emma Gage-Echo," Tate whispered. "One of these days, I'm going to convince you that we belong together. Even walls fall down sometimes, Em. Even walls."

About the Author

Tammy Cheatham grew up in rural East Texas and learned to love books and reading at an early age. Her writing career began in the fifth grade when she won second place in a UIL writing contest but was put on hold while she pursued a career and raised a family. With her three children grown, Tammy elected to retire from her full time job and return to her first career choice, writing fiction. Today, Tammy lives in South Texas near San Antonio with her husband.

www.ingramcontent.com/pod-product-compliance
Lightning Source LLC
Chambersburg PA
CBHW020556180626
46810CB00007B/2530